THE AWAKENING OF JAPAN

OKAKURA·KAKUZO

CONTENTS

PUBLISHERS' PREFACE ix

CHAPTER I. THE NIGHT OF ASIA

    The sudden development of Japan an enigma to foreign observers — Asia the true source of Japan's inspiration — While Christendom struggled with medievalism the Buddhaland was a garden of culture — Effect of Islam upon Asia — The Mongol outburst destroyed Asia's unity — The condition of China and India — Japan never conquered, but buried alive for nearly 270 years 3

CHAPTER II. THE CHRYSALIS

    Japan under the Tokugawa shogunate — Iyeyasu's influence — The Mikado's palace the "Forbidden Interior" — The kuges, or court aristocracy — The daimios — The samurai, or sworded gentry — The commoners: farmers, artisans, and traders — The outcasts — The nation in a pleasant slumber 22

CHAPTER III. BUDDHISM AND CONFUCIANISM

    Buddhism and Confucianism never interfered in matters of state — Despite its temples and monasteries, Japan has no church — Neo-Confucianism 53

CHAPTER IV. THE VOICE FROM WITHIN

    Three schools of thought united in causing the regeneration of Japan — First, the Kogaku, or School of Classical Learning — Second, the School of Oyomei — Third, the Historical School 70

PUBLISHERS' PREFACE

Okakura-Kakuzo, the author of this work and of " The Ideals of the East," was born in the year 1863. Having been, as he has said, " from early youth fond of old things," after leaving college in 1880 he interested himself in the formation of clubs and societies for ar-chseological research. The Japanese Renaissance, begun at the end of the eighteenth century, suffered a brief check during the civil commotion following the opening of the country after the arrival of the American Commodore Perry. The work of Okakura was a resumption of that begun by the earlier scholars.

In 1886 this scholarly young enthusiast was sent to America and Europe as a commissioner to report on Western art education. On returning, he organ-ix
ized the Imperial Art School of Tokio, of which he was made director. He was also one of the chief organizers, and is still a member, of the Imperial Archaeological Commission, w^hose duty it is to study, classify, and preserve the ancient architecture, the archives of the monasteries, and all specimens of ancient art.

Okakura was, naturally, one of the promoters of the reactionary movement against the wholesale introduction of Western art and manners. This movement was carried on by the starting of periodicals and clubs devoted to the preservation of the old life of Japan,— the work being carried on, also, in the field of literature and the drama.

In 1898 he resigned the directorship of the Imperial Art School at Tokio, having had some difference -with the educational authorities in the matter of the course of instruction to be pursued therein. Nearly one half of the faculty resigned at the same time, and started, in a suburb of Tokio, a private academy called Nippon Bijitsuin. Here are kept up the ancient traditions of native art.

Simultaneously with the foundation of this school of instruction, a number of prominent painters of the national school of art in various parts of the country organized the Society of Japanese Painters, of which the president is Prince Nijo,—the head of the Fujiwara family and uncle of the crown princess,—Okakura being elected vice-president.

It is proper to state that the present work, like " The Ideals of the East," is not a translation, but is written by its Japanese author originally in English. This work is based not merely upon printed material and common hearsay, but upon information derived through the author's special acquaintance with surviving actors in the Restoration.

In " The Awakening of Japan " the author answers with profound knowledge, great vividness of expression, and
intense patriotism the question now uppermost in the minds of Western observers : From what sources are drawn the intellectual and moral qualities which have enabled the present generation of statesmen, citizens, soldiers, and sailors, under an able emperor, to enter suddenly, as a fii'st-class liberal power, into the company of nations?

The author shows clearly and picturesquely that the accomplishments of the New Japan are the natural outcome of her history,—her religion, her art, her tradition. He declares that there is no " Yellow Peril"; that the empire, though warlike, stands not for aggression but for peace! He sketches the entire history of the country, but dwells particularly upon modern events and developments,—the opening of the long-closed door of the imprisoned nation by Commodore

Perry, the restoration of the Mikado to power, the new regime, the occasion of the war of 1904. He essays an answer to the anxious query of the admirers of the art of Japan: Will Japan's modern successes lead to the loss of its ancient and distinctive art? He indicates some of the tendencies which may affect the future of the Orient; and he speaks especially of the Christian attitude toward woman as an influence upon the society and civilization of Japan.

THE AWAKENING OF JAPAN

THE NIGHT OF ASIA

THE sudden development of Japan has been more or less of an enigma to foreign observers. She is the country of flowers and ironclads, of dashing heroism and delicate tea-cups,—the strange borderland where quaint shad'-ows cross each other in the twilight of the New and the Old World. Until recently the West has never taken Japan seriously. It is amusing to find nowadays that such success as we have achieved in our efforts to take a place among the family of nations appears in the eyes of many as a menace to Christendom. In the mysterious nothing is improbable. Exaggeration is the courtesy which fancy pays to the unknown. What sweeping condemnation, what absurd praise has not the world lavished on New Japan? We are both the cherished child of modern progress and a dread resurrection of heathendom—the Yellow Peril itself!

Has not the West as much to unlearn about the East as the East has to learn about the West? In spite of the vast sources of information at the command of the West, it is sad to realize to-day how many misconceptions are still entertained concerning us. We do not mean to allude to the unthinking masses who are still dominated by race prejudice and that vague hatred of the Oriental which is a relic from the days of the crusades. But even the comparatively well-informed fail to recognize the inner significance of our revival and the real goal of our aspirations. It may be that, as our problems have been none of the simplest, our attitude has been often paradoxical. Perhaps the fact that the history of East Asiatic civilization is still a sealed book to the Western public may account for the great variety of opinions held by the outside world concerning our present conditions and future possibilities.

Our sympathizers have been pleased to marvel at the facility with which we have introduced Western science and industries, constitutional government, and the organization necessary for carrying on a gigantic war. They forget that the strength of the movement which brought Japan to her present position is due not less to the innate viriHty which has enabled her to assimilate the teachings of a foreign civilization than to her capability of adopting its methods. With a race,] as with the individual, it is not the ac- 1 cumulation of extraneous knowledge, I but the realization of the self within, I that constitutes true progress. ""

With immense gratitude to the West for what she has taught us, we must still regard Asia as the true source of our inspirations. She it was who transmitted to us her ancient culture, and planted the seed of our regeneration. Our joy must be in the fact that, of all her children, we have been permitted to prove ourselves worthy of the inheritance. Great as was the difficulty

involved in the struggle for a national reawakening, a still harder task confronted Japan in her effort to bring an Oriental nation to face the terrible exigencies, of modern existence. Until the moment when we shook it off, the same lethargy lay upon us which now lies on China and India. Over our"^ country brooded the Night of Asia, en-] veloping all spontaneity within its mysterious folds. Intellectual activity and social progress became stifled in the atmosphere of apathy. Religion could but soothe, not cure, the suffering of the wounded soul. The weight of our burden can never be understood without a knowledge of the dark background from which we emerged to the light.

The decadence of Asia began long ago with the Mongol conquest in the

thirteenth century. The classic civilizations of China and India shine the brighter by contrast with the night that has overtaken them since that disastrous irruption. The children of the Hwang-ho and the Ganges had from early days evolved a culture comparable with that of the era of highest enlightenment in Greece and Rome, one which even foreshadowed the trend of advanced thought in modern Europe. Buddhism, introduced into China and the farther East during the early centuries of the Christian era, bound together the Vedic and Confucian ideals in a single web, and brought about the unification of Asia. A vast stream of intercoui'se flowed throughout the extent of the whole Buddhaland. Tidings of any fresh philosophical achievement in the University of Nalanda,^ or in

1 The center of Buddhist learning in Behar.

the monasteries of Kashmir, were brought by pilgrims and wandering monks to the thought-centers of China^ Korea, and Japan. Kingdoms often exchanged courtesies, while peace married art to art. From this synthesis of the whole Asiatic life a fresh impetus was given to each nation. It is curious to note that each eiFort in one nation to attain a higher expression of humanity is marked by a simultaneous and parallel movement in the other. That liber.Mism and magnificence, resulting in the worship of poetry and harmony, which, in the sixth century, so characterized the reign of Vikra-maditya in India, appear equally in the glorious age of the Tang emperors of China (618-907), and at the court of our contemporary mikados at Nara. Again the movement toward individualism and renationalization which, in the

eighth century, is marked in India by the advent of Sankaracharya, the apostle of

Hinduism, is followed, during the Sung dynasty (960-1260), by a similar activity in China, culminating in Neo-Confucianism and the recasting of the Zen school ^ of Buddhism, a phase echoed both in Japan and Korea. Thus, while Christendom was struggling with medievalism, the Buddha-land was a great garden of culture, where each flower of thought bloomed in individual beauty.

But, alas! the Mongol horsemen under Jenghiz Khan were to lay waste these areas of civilization, and make of them a desert like that out of which they themselves came. It was not the first time that the warriors of the steppes

Zen is the sect of Buddhism which seeks illumination through self-concentration. It corresponds to the Indian Gnan.

THE NIGHT OF ASIA

had appeared in the rich valleys of China and India. The Huns and the Scythians had often succeeded in temporarily inflicting their rule on the borders of these countries. After a time, however, they were either driven out, or else tamed and finally absorbed in the peaceful life of the plain. But this last Mongol outburst was of a magnitude unequaled in the past. It was destined not only to reach the Pacific and the Indian Ocean, but to cross the Ural and overflow Moscow. The descendants of Jenghiz Khan in China established the Yuen dynasty and reigned at Peking from 1280 to 1368, while their cousins began a series of attacks on India which ended in the empire of the Grand Moguls. The Yuens still adhered to Buddhism, though in the degenerate form known 11

THE AWAKENING OF JAPAN

as Lamaism; but the Mogul emperors of Delhi, who came in the footsteps of Mahmud of Ghazni, had embraced the Arabian faith as they sped on their path of conquest through southern Asia. The Moguls not only-exterminated Buddhism, but also persecuted Hinduism. It was a terrible blow to Buddlialand when Islam interposed a barrier between China and India greater than the Himalayas themselves. The flow of intercourse, so essential to human progress, was suddenly stopped. Our own time-honored relations with our continental neighbors even began to wane after the Mongol conquerors of China attempted to invade Japan in the latter part of the thirteenth centuiy, forcing Korea to act as their ally. Their belligerent attitude continued for nearly 12

THE NIGHT OF ASIA

forty years; and though, thanks to our insular position and the prowess of our warriors, we were able successfully to repel their attacks, remembrance of their aggression was not to be effaced, and even led to retaliatory steps on our part. The memory of our ancient friendship with the courts of the Tang and Sung dynasties was lost. One of the latent causes of our late war with the Celestial Empire 'may be found in the mutual suspicion with which the two nations have now regarded each other for many centuries. By the]Mongol conquest of Asia, Buddlialand was rent asunder, never again to be reunited. How little do the Asiatic nations now know of each other! They have grown callous to the doom that befalls their neighbors.

One cannot but be struck by the con-13

THE AWAKENING OF JAPAN

trast between the effect of the Mongol outburst on Buddhaland and Christendom. The maritime races of the Mediterranean and the Baltic, by their long course of mutual aggression, were well equipped to cope with the terrific onslaught of the nomadic invaders. In spite of temporary reverses, Europe may even be said to have gained some advantage from those struggles which were so disastrous to us of the East. It was then that she first developed that power of combination which makes her so formidable to-day. The Mongol outburst, which displaced the Turkish hordes and resulted in the creation of the Saracenic and Ottoman empires, gave the Frankish nations the opportunity of uniting against a common enemy. Before the walls of Jerusalem and on the banks of the Danube met in

comradeship, once and forever, the flower of Christian chivahy, and there was consolidated a conception of Christendom such as papal Rome could never alone have brought into existence. The fall of Constantinople was in itself one of the chief factors of the Italian Renaissance.

The peaceful and self-contained nature of Eastern civilization has been ever weak to resist foreign aggression. We have not only permitted the ^Mon-gol to destroy the unity of Asia, but have allowed him to crush the life of Indian and Chinese culture. From both the thrones of Peking and Delhi, the descendants of Jenghiz Khan perpetuated a system of despotism contrary to the traditional policies of the lands they had subjugated. Entire lack of sympathy between the con-

querors and the conquered, the introduction of an alien official language, the refusal to the native of any vital participation in administration, together with the dreadful clash of race-ideals and religious beliefs, all combined to produce a mental shock and anguish of spirit from which the Indians and the Chinese have never recovered. Su-^h scholarship as was allowed to survive, was confined to those servile minds who submitted meekly to barbaric patronage. What was left of original intellectual vigor was heard only among the despairing echoes of the forest, or in the savage laughter of the bazaar. Art thenceforth becomes either ultra-conventional or else bizarre and grotesque.

Attempts to overthrow the foreign yoke were not lacking, and some of

them were even successful. But the disintegration of the national consciousness under alien tyranny made renationalization almost impossible, and the native dynasties were unable to withstand fresh waves of outside aggression. In China, the Ming or Bright dynasty, which wrested the government from the Mongols in the middle of the fourteenth century, soon became a prej^ to internal discords. Scarcely had the destruction attendant on the Mongol reign been repaired, when, near the end of the sixteenth century, a fresh invasion came from the north, and the Manchus tore the scepter from the native rulers. In spite of the strenuous efforts made by the wiser statesmen of this new dynasty, no complete fusion of the Manchus and the Chinese has ever been accomplished.

To-day the Celestial Empire is so divided against itself that it is powerless to repel outside attack. Europe, with her iron grasp on some of her most important ports, has even contemplated the partition of the whole of China. So in India the reactionary uprising of the Mahrattas and the Sikhs against the Mohammedan tyrants, though partially successful, did not crystallize into a universal expression of patriotism. This lack of unity enabled a Western power to shape her destinies.

Bereft of the spirit of initiative, tired of impotent revolts, and deprived of legitimate ambitions, the Chinese and the Indian of to-day have come to prostrate themselves before the inevitable. Some among them find refuge in the memory of past grandeur, thus hardening the crust of tradition and exclusiveness; 18

THE NIGHT OF ASIA

while the souls of others, wafted among ethereal dreams, seek solace in an appeal to the unknown. The Night of Asia, which enshrouds them, is not, perhaps, without its own subtle beauty. It reminds us of the deep glorious nights we know so well in the East,— listless like wonder, serene like sadness, opalescent like love. One may touch the stars behind the veil where man meets spirit. One may listen to the secret cadence of nature beyond the border where sound bows to silence.

Japan, who had proved herself equal to the task of repelling the Mongol invasion, found little difficulty in resisting that attempt at Western encroachment which, at the beginning of the seventeenth century, came in the form of the Shimabara Rebellion, instigated by the Jesuits. It has been 19

THE AWAKENING OF JAPAN

our boast that no foreign conqueror ,ever polluted the soil of Japan, but these attempts at aggression from the outside hardened our insular prejudice into a desire for complete isolation ; from the rest of the world. Soon after the Jesuit war the building of vessels large enough to ride the high seas was forbidden, and no one was allowed to leave our shores. Our sole point of contact with the outside world was at the port of Nagasaki, where the Chinese and the Dutch were permitted, under strict surveillance, to carry on ti-ade. For the space of nearly two hundred and sevent\'7d^ years we were as one buried alive!

Yet a worse fate was in store for us.
The Tokugawa shoguns, who brought
about this remarkable isolation of
Japan, ruled the country from 1600 to

THE NIGHT OF ASIA

1868, and threw the invisible network of their tyranny over all the nation. From the highest to the lowest, all were entangled in a subtle web of mutual espionage, and every element of individuality was crushed under the weight of unbending formalism. Deprived of all stimulus from without, and imprisoned within, our own island realm groped amid a maze of tradition. Darkest over us lay the Night of Asia.

THE CHRYSALIS

THE Tokugawa tyrants, who initiated the policy of strict seclusion, were the successors of various lines of shoguns who, as military regents of the INIikado, had, since the twelfth century, usurped the government of Japan. Before that period, Japan was under the personal rule of the Mikado, who, with the assistance of court functionaries, reigned over the country from Kioto. The over-centralization of the imperial bureaucracy, however, was the cause of its own decay. Its neglect of provincial administration led to local disturbances and the creation of baronial es-

tales, over which the Kioto court exercised no active control. The real authority thus came into the hands of the strongest baronial power, whose representative, vested by the ^likado with the title of shogun, or commander-in-chief, ruled the country as regent, the Mikado retaining but a nominal sovereignty over the empire.

The first, or Kamakura, shogunate, so called from the city which its representatives made their capital, exercised the powers of government from 1186 to 1333. This was followed by a temporary restitution of power to the Mikado ; but the reins of government soon fell into the hands of another line of shoguns, the Ashikaga. who from 1336 to 1573 ruled the country from Kioto itself. The fall of the Ashikaga shogunate was followed by a long period

of civil war, during which the various great barons struggled for supremacy. Out of this state of turmoil arose that Napoleonic genius, Taiko Hideyoshi, who, born a peasant, died, in 1598, the master of unified Japan. His son was, however, unable to retain the authority left him by his father, and the dictatorship of the empire devolved, in 1600, on lyeyasu, the fii*st of the Tokugawa shoguns.

The Tokugawa shogunate differed from those preceding it in that it was virtually a monarchy, despite its apparent feudalistic fomi. Even under the great Taiko, the government of the country was conducted by a council composed of five of the most powerful barons, but under the Tokugawa regime it became purely autocratic. lyeyasu framed for his descendants a

course of policy which enabled them to retain their rule through fourteen generations, until the recent restoration of the Mikado in 1868. He not merely curtailed the power of the barons until they were such only in name, but erected safeguards against every possible source of danger to his dynasty. He not only cut us off from all outside intercourse, but so separated the different classes of society, that the idea of national unity became completely lost. The subtleness of his machinations is manifest not less in his elaborate scheme for maintaining military ascendancy than in the way in which he took advantage of our own idiosyncrasies and secret vanities to disarm all opposition to his rule. In order that he might yoke us unresistingly to the car of routine, he soothed our feelings and

delighted our souls by appeals to that love and worship for the past that is one of our national instincts. Our bonds were, in fact, largely of our own weaving, and lyeyasu but lulled us to sleep, unmindful of the future, within the chrysalis of tradition. Perhaps it is for this, that he knew us only too well, we execrate his memory to-day.

The mechanism of the Tokugawa rule cannot be adequately described in brief; not only is it exceedingly complicated, but it is without striking parallel in the history of any country. It affords the peculiar spectacle of a society perfectly isolated and self-complete, which, acting and reacting upon itself, produced worlds within worlds, each with its separate life and ideals, and its own distinct expressions in art and literature. It exhibits all the subtleness of European class distinction, plus the element of caste as understood in India. We can here but indicate its main phases.

First, over all was the Mikado. That sacred conception is the thought-inheritance of Japan from her very beginning. M>thology has consecrated it, history has ct deared it, and poetry has idealized it. Buddhism has enriched it with that reverence which India pays to the " Protector of the Law," and Confucianism has confirmed it with the loyalty which China offers to the " Son of Heaven." The Mikado may cease to govern, but he always reigns. He exists not by divine right, but bj^ divine law,—a fact of man and nature. He is always there, like our beloved mountain of Fuji, which stands eternally in silent

beauty, or like the glorious sea which forever washes our shore.

We must remember, however, that the political significance of the Mikado has not always been the same. As we are often unconscious of the every-day facts of nature, because of their unquestioned existence, so we became unconscious of the Mikado, and basked in the daylight, unmindful of the sun above. Clouds of successive usurpations long obscured the heavens, so that devotion to the Solar Throne became a distant though never entirely forgotten homage. By the sixteenth century, when Iyeyasu assumed the shogunate and became in reality absolute monarch of Japan, all memory of the personal rule of the Mikado had been lost for four long centuries. The Mikado's court at Kioto, the fomier capital of the imperial government, was still existent, owing to its past prestige, but it was only a faint reflection of its former glory.

The great genius of Iyeyasu is apparent in his full recognition of the Mikado in the national scheme. In strong contrast to the arrogance and utter neglect which the preceding shoguns displayed toward the court, he spared no effort to show his respect. He augmented the imperial revenues, invited the daimios (feudal lords) to participate in rebuilding the imperial palace, restored the court ceremonial and etiquette, and was unceasing in his ministrations to the welfare of the imperial household. He even started the unprecedented ceremony of the sho-gun paying personal homage to the throne, and a brilliant pageant yearly passed from his castle of Yeddo (now kno^vn as Tokio), dazzling the delighted ej^es of the populace as it wended its way slowly toward Kioto. All this was flattering to the national love of tradition. It was considered as heralding the advent of the millennium.

But behind this appearance of loyalty to the throne lay liidden the subtlest snares of the Tokugawas. If they recognized the necessity of the imperial cult, they determined that they alone should be its high-priests, and that others should worship at a respectful distance. In the name of sanctity, the Kioto court was deprived of those last remnants of political authority which former regencies had suiFered it to retain. A strong garrison was stationed in Kioto, ostensibly for the protection of the palace,])iit its members were chosen from the tried body-guard of the Tokugawas themselves. They continued to invite one of the imperial princes to take the monastic vows and reside in Yeddo as lord abbot of the Uyeno temple, by which means they always virtually held at their capital a hostage from the Kioto court. No daimio was allowed to seek audience of the]Mikado without their consent.

The Mikado, unseen and unheard, commanded a mysterious awe. His palace now became the "Forbidden Interior" in the strict sense of the word. The ancient political significance of the court was lost in a semi-religious conception. No wonder that the Westerners who first visited our country wrote that there were two rulers in Japan, the temporal in Yeddo, and the spiritual in Kioto. In spite of the constant loyalty which our forefathers expressed for the Mikado in Tokugawa days, they had none of the fiery enthusiasm which inspires us to-day. With them it was symbolism; with us it is a living reality.

Next to the Mikado, and foremost in social rank (the imperial line being considered above all class distinctions), came the kuges, or court aristocracy of Kioto. The exalted position which they held in society arose from their association with the Mikado. From their position near the throne, they were called poetically the Friends of the Moon and Guests of the Cloud. Their fortunes waxed and waned with those of the imperial household, to which, regardless of the immense political changes that have come over Japan since the days when they actively participated in the conduct of the empire, they have ever remained faithful. Herein again lies another remarkable example of that obstinate tenacity which makes the Japanese race preserve the old while it welcomes the new. The kuges were the successors of those princely bureaucrats who participated in the imperial rule from the year 645 to 1166. The old system of government, together with its social customs and art expressions, was based mainly on that of the Tang dynasty of China. The kuges have always remained guardians of its ideals. While China was trying one policy after another, and Japan herself was passing through various different phases of feudalism toward the monarchism of the Tokugawas, the kuges continued to live the life which preceded the twelfth century. Their costumes were of the eleventh, their etiquette of the tenth century. They read Chinese with the intonation of the Tang period, and danced to the classic measure of the Bugaku music, the inheritance of an era preceding the ninth century. They delighted in the purism of the Fujiwara poetry, and affected the technic of the ancient school of painting. It is to their devotion to the past that we owe the preservation of the Kharma-kanda (ritualistic observances) of India and the early Buddhist doctrines of China.

The Tokugawa government humored and honored the court nobles because of their association with the Mikado and the place they occupied in the history of the nation. The kuges were given precedence over the daimios, and their incomes, if not greatly increased, were at least assured to them. This last must have been gratifying to those of them who remembered the disastrous days when they had to sell autograph poems for their sustenance. They were contented, and the Tokugawas kept them well disposed toward themselves by intermarriage and timely financial aid. All political power, however, was completely taken from the kuges, notwithstanding the high-sounding titles which they were still allowed to retain. The duty of the privy councilor would consist in debating on the merits of a love-ditty, and that of the high minister of state in presiding over a competition of nightingales. It was in those days of refined folly that the queen in our game of chess was solemnly abolished by imperial command. Theoretically, next to the court nobility of Kioto in social position, but actually far prouder and more powerful, came the daimios, or feudal lords (literally grandees), nearly three hundred in number. These were divided into classes—the Tozama daimios, who were the descendants of the barons of former days, and the daimios of recent creation, who had been ennobled by the Tokugawas, either for their services, or because they traced their lineage tc some member of that famJly. In the early days of Tokugawa rule, the Tozama daimios were a source of great danger, as their ancient warlike spirit remained as yet untamed. The methods that lyeyasu and his successors employed in maintaining military ascendancy, and in generally bringing the daimios under absolute control, are a study in themselves. Any map of Japan

in the early days of the Tokugawas will show the feudatory provinces so distributed that all political combination between them was rendered impossible. On such a map we will find the daimi-ates of Tokugawa creation, which were constantly being augmented in size and strength, wedged in between the earlier daimiates. Gradually all strategical points on the main roads of communication throughout the country were taken from the Tozama daimios, and either held by the shogun himself or put into the hands of his minions. The practice of assembling the daimios at Yeddo to sit in conference over questions of territorial rights soon led to the inauguration of a system bj'^ which each daimio was obliged to leave his territory every alternate year and pay personal homage to the shogun, while his

family were required to reside permanently at the capital as hostages. In this manner the greater part of such time as the daimios were not under immediate control of the shogun w^as consumed in journeying to and from their provinces, so that but little opportunity was given them to form or carry out conspiracies against the government. The newly enacted law of inheritance demanded the approval of the government in each case of succession to the daimiates, and also in all cases of marriage. A constant drain was maintained on their feudatory income by inviting the daimios to assist in repairing the imperial palace, and in other public works. Jealousj^ and rivalry were encouraged to such an extent that they resulted in a lamentable condition of mutual distrust and espionage.

Those Tozama daimios who revolted against this state of things soon found out their impotence, and were invariably punished by the diminution, transference, or confiscation of their territorial possessions,—the latter penalty attended with death. They were taught to realize that the government of the country, though still feudal in form, had become in reahty an absolute monarchy,—patriarchal and benevolent, but thoroughly despotic. They soon found that their smallest actions were watched with unceasing vigilance, so that they began to be distrustful of even their own retainers. This vigorous surveillance was not confined to the Tozama daimios alone. Dreading the combination of administrative power with hereditary influence, the Tokugawas invariably chose their cab-

inet ministers from among the smaller daimios of their own creation. The powerful members of their own aristocracy were watched as strictly as were the Tozama lords, a fact which explains why all the daimios were so lukewarm in their sympathy toward the Tokugawa government during the struggles of the Restoration.

Below the daimios came the samurai, or sworded gentry, four hundred thousand strong. They served either immediately under the shogun himself, or else under the banners of the various daimios. Their appointments w^ere hereditary, and their blood was kept pure by the prohibition of all marriage with the lower classes, except in case of the foot-soldiers, who constituted the lowest rank of samurai. They had the right and obligation of wearing two swords and bearing family crests. Within their own ranks were many class distinctions, each with its special privileges. The estates of high-class samurai were often wider and richer than those of the smaller daimios. Under the code of the samurai, however, all enjoyed that equality that belongs to comradeship in arms; and even as a king of England or France delighted in the title of first gentleman of the land, so the shogun considered himself first samurai of the empire.

But with the advent of the Toku-gawa regime the existence of the dai-mio and the samurai, like that of the court aristocracy of Kioto, became an anachronism. The samurai, a product of the feudal period intervening between the fall of the imperial bureaucracy in the twelfth century and the rise of the Tokugawa monarchy in the seventeenth century, clung with singular tenacity to their past ideals. Their art was that of the Kano school, a reflection of the fifteenth century. Their music and drama were the No, the sixteenth-century opera of Japan. Their costumes, architecture, and language retained the style of the time immediately preceding the Tokugawa period. Their religion followed those Zen doctrines which had been the vital inspiration of the feudal age. In fact, the whole code of the samurai was an heirloom left to them by the Kama-kura and Ashikaga knights, in whose days the whole nation was a camp.

Iyeyasu, accepting Japan as it was, and utilizing its idiosyncrasies, kept the military class quiet through its own love of hereditary conventions and military obedience. Everything was regulated by precedent and routine. The son of a samurai or a daimio followed exactly in the footsteps of his father, and dreamed of no change. By giving the samm-ai a Confucian education, the Tokugawas both pacified his warlike instincts and encouraged his worship of tradition. The blessing of that rule which they termed the Great Peace of Tokugawa was so constantly dinned into his ears that he hoped and believed that it would be everlasting.

The life of a Tokugawa daimio or samurai was not devoid of amusements. Besides his fencing-bouts and jiujitsu matches, his falconry and games of archery, he had his No-dances, his tea-ceremonies, and those interminable banquets at which he would recount the exploits of his ancestors. Moreover, much time might be consumed in the composition of bad Chinese poems beneath the cherry-trees. He was often wealthy and always extravagant, for his contempt for gold was ingrained. He would squander a fortune for a rare Sung vase or a Masamune blade. The marvelous workmanship of the Gotos in metal, and of the Komas in gold lacquer was the result of his patronage. It is to the disappearance of the daimio and the samurai that Japan owes her sudden fall of standard in artistic taste.

Such samurai as had been thrown out of employment either through dismissal by their lord or the extinction of the daimiate under which they served, were called ronin (the unattached). Sometimes a second son, with literary talents or scholastic ambitions, became a ronin, and supported himself by teaching. The ronins retained all the rights and privileges of the samurai, while their state of independence gave them an individuality and freedom of thought unknown among their more orthodox brethren. It was through the ronin scholars that the first message of the Restoration was to be announced to the nation.

Fourth in the social scale came the commoners, ranked in the order of farmers, artisans, and traders. As in the case of the rise of European monarchies the populace ever came to the help of the sovereign against the nobles, so in Japan the Tokugawas found in the commoners their best allies against the daimios, and consequently granted them many privileges hitherto unknown. Then life and prop-

erty of the masses found a security unprecedented in the days of the predatory barons. Within a limited sphere, they were even allowed to develop self-government. Industry and commerce flourished unmolested. Agriculture was specially encouraged, as rice was the medium in which the revenues of the government were taken. It is to the commoners that we owe the arts and , crafts which have made Japan famous. • ' It is to them that we are indebted for our modern drama and popular literature, the color-prints of Torii and Ho-kusai.

Toward the conmioners also, however, the Tokugawas pursued their policy of segregation, inclosing them by barriers of tradition within a separate compartment of their social structure. They were welcome to their spe-

cial vocations and amusements, but they were forbidden to trespass on what belonged to the higher orders. They were not allowed to wear family crests, or even to bear surnames. They could have their theater, with its line of dangiuros (actors), but might not indulge in the no-mus'ic of the samurai, or the classic dance of the Kioto no-. bihty.

As a precaution against an uprising, all the commoners were disarmed. An immense body of secret police was employed to watch their movements, and any breath of discontent met with severe punishment. Silent fear haunted them, for all the walls seemed to have grown ears. Theirs it was to work and obey, and not to question. However rich or accomplished, commoners born must die commoners. Henmied in by

inexorable customs and restrictions, their energy had to vent itself either through the frivolity of life or the sadness of religion. Can we wonder that to the more serious commoners religion consisted in an appeal to the infinite mercy of Amitaba for absorption in that divine love, the expression of which is so marked in the Bhaktas of India? Can we blame the weaker and more frivolous among them for seeking forgetfulness in the idealization of folly?

Below the commoners, and, in fact, ostracized entirely from the social scheme, were the outcasts known as Yettas. They were the descendants of criminals, who, in early times, were not allowed to intermarry with other families, and so formed a distinct caste by themselves. Some of them became

quite wealthy, owing to their possession of a monopoly in the handling of leather and hide, an occujiation considered unclean, according to the Buddhist canons. It was from their ranks that the public executioners were appointed. Before the Restoration, when all men were made equal in the eye of the law, any contact with this class was considered a pollution.

The national consciousness, divided within itself by the dams and dikes of its own conventions, could but narrow and finally stagnate. The flow of spontaneity ceased with the end of the seventeenth century. The microscopic tendency of later Oriental thought became in us accentuated to a degree unknown even in China. Our life grew to be like those miniature and dwarf trees that were typical products of the Tokugawa age. Alone in the field of art and literature, essentially the world of freedom, some vitality is to be found. The self-concentration of a nation during that period has given a peculiar charm to Japanese art. The worship of traditions, which is the foundation of style and elegance, has given a subtle refinement to all its expressions. Yet this very classicism was the enemy of the romanticist efforts, for true individuality was subdued under the general trend of formalism. Again, the demarcation of social life and ideals prevented any creative mind from mirroring the whole of national loves and aspirations. Despite a certain cleverness in details, or an occasional dash of wild fancy, no painter of the caliber of Korin,[1] or poet with the strength of Chikamatsu,[1] is to be found. Some, like beautiful pools, may reflect the shadows of contemporary thought; but in not one do we get a vision of the limitless ocean of the ideal.

[1] Korin, a great colorist in the latter half of the seventeenth century,

Yet the hibernation of Japan within her chrysalis must have been pleasant in itself, or the nation would not have slumbered so long. Old folks are still to be found who cherish the memory of those days of leisure, when no one was so vulgar as to think for himself, when life was elegant, if it was formal. There were always chances of being exquisitely foolish, if one was wise enough to avail himself of them. Said Kampici, the Chinese Machiavelli, in telling the secret of absolutism twenty-two centuries ago: "Amuse them, tire them not, let them not know." Iyeyasu, a past master of craft, followed these injunctions but too faithfully. We were amused, we cared not for change, we did not seek to know.

[1] Chikamatsu, his contemporary, the Japanese Shakspere.

BUDDHISM AND CONFUCIANISM

SOME critics see in the encouragement given to learning that flaw in the Tokugawa system of government which caused its ultimate downfall. Under the regime inaugurated by Iyeyasu every child in the empire was obliged to learn to read and write, under the instruction of the local priests, thus giving a certain amount of education to even the meanest peasant, while innumerable academies were established throughout the length and breadth of the land. It is doubtless true that the result of these measures was to prepare the national mind for receiving the message of the Restoration. Yet, when we come to examine into the nature of the instruction so freely given to the people by the Tokugawas, we shall find that perhaps Iyeyasu and his immediate successors were not so far amiss in their calculations, after all.

All branches of knowledge are interesting, but some courses of study tend to encourage ignorance, and such were the courses in Buddliism and Confucianism which formed the sole curriculum in the Tokugawa academies. To those who have seen our landscapes studded with pagodas, and heard our temple bells calling from every hill, or to those who remember the great halls of learning in the various daimiates, and the chant of reciting voices in every Tokugawa village, it must seem strange that Buddhism and Confucianism played so small a part in the Restoration. The fact is that their teachings never interfered in matters of state, and their influence was solely directed toward enforcing ideas of submission and the love of peace.

We do not agree with those enemies of Iyeyasu - who accuse liim of being a skeptic and utilizing ethics and religion only as a means to further his own ends. He was a great statesman who combined many of the characteristics of Cromwell and Richelieu. He was sincere, and acted, according to his lights, for what he considered the best interests of the nation. The following instance of his humanity is enough to refute those charges of heartlessness which have been brought against him. Noticing, during one of his campaigns, that the enemy were using loose-shafted arrows, the heads of which remained in the wound and caused a cruel and lingering death, he gave orders that all the Tokugawa arrowheads should be securely fastened and lacquered to the shafts. We believe, however, that the "Old Badger," as he is often nicknamed, knew full well the nature of Buddhist and Confucian teaching, and that his astuteness and knowledge of men did not fail to recognize the bearing which the Oriental philosophy of his day might have upon the furtherance of his system of government.

Buddhism was never a menace to the state. The reason for this lies far back in the antithesis of the Oriental conception of the social and supersocial order. By that antithesis the ethical life of the householder is distinguished from the religious life of the wandering recluse, the two standing in contrast, though not necessarily antagonistic. Eastern society, with all its beauty of harmonized duties and intercalated occupations, is based on mutual dependencies, and at best can but end in conventionalism—the moral bondage of the commune. Religion, on the other hand, furnishes the means of true emancipation, and constitutes the acme of individualism. The ideal monk is the child of freedom, who, dying to the mundane, is reborn to the realm of the spirit. He is like the lotus which rises in purity above the mire. He is silent, like the forest in which he meditates; untrammeled, like the wind that blows his gown around him. He is of no caste and no country. What if thrones are overthrown and nations enslaved: did not Buddha, the great teacher of renunciation, watch with undimmed eyes the total annihilation of his own kingly race?

Society, the world of tradition and ethics, looked with respect on the world of freedom, and gazed with wonder at the achievements of the spiritual workers who left behind them the boundary lines of school and sect as they traveled through the regions of the unexplored toward the light. Chinese mandarins dreamed, amid palatial luxuries, of the bamboo forest, and sighed at the call of the pine-clad hills. The highest desire of an Indian or Japanese householder was to reach the age at which, leaving worldly cares to his children, he might learn that higher life of a recluse known as Banaprasta or Inkyo. In donning the monkish robe, a privilege open to all, he found release from the world of convention. It was in order to escape from social trammels that our artists shaved their heads and assumed the guise of priests.

But the social and the supersocial worlds never clashed, for each was the counterpart of the other. In Indian society we find the Shramanic as the necessary counterbalance to the Brahmanic ideal, while in China the same positions are held by Taoism and Confucianism. Herein lies the secret of that toleration which has made of India a rouseum of religions, and has caused China to welcome, so long as they do not interfere with her political system, the alien faiths of Buddhism, Zoroastrianism, Nestorianism, Mohammedanism, and modern Christianity. The existence of this twofold development also explains, in a certain measure, that attitude of liberalism and apparent indifference which our modern statesmen of Japan display toward religious questions,—an attitude often construed as a false idea of European statecraft, if not of agnosticism. The demarcation of the political from the religious life, the divorce of state and church, is no new idea with us. Indeed, despite our temples and monasteries, we have no church.

The innate individualism of the Buddhist ideal, unlike that of the papal church of Europe, which is even now a source of concern to some nations, has ever prevented the formation of a single powerful organization to impose its influej;ice on the state. The temporal power exercised by some of our monks was due solely to their personal influence over the Mikado or his officers, in the imperial days before the feudal period. It was a sort of mundane offering laid at the feet of holiness, and was the temporary result of a purely personal relationship. The priesthood, as a body or sect, rarely tried to retain authority over the govermnent, and the social consciousness was always eager to reclaim what it considered its own special function. A sovereign might be carried away by his sjjiritual zeal, but the dynasty invariably recovered its equilibrium. With the rise of the Ka-makura shogunate, the Buddhist power, which had its root in the devotion of the Kioto court, declined. The ultra-individualistic sect of Zen, which at this time became the leading school of thought, made no pretense to political-ambition. During the turbulent age that followed, the predatory attacks of neighboring barons on the monasteries caused the establishment of an armed monkliood. These warrior-priests guarded the sanctuaries, and, either alone or in alliance with various dai-mios, were a prominent feature in the Ashikaga wars, where they are often found foremost in the fray, their robe of mercy ill concealing the bloodstained mail beneath. They had, however, almost disappeared by the time of lyeyasu, when the Hongangi, the last sect which still boasted of some military adherents, was easily made to submit to the authority of the shogun.

The policy of lyeyasu toward Buddhism is characteristic of the fundamental idea of Eastern statesmanship. Himself a Confucian, he counted among his best friends the three great Buddhist monks of his age. He would have tolerated even Christianity, if the Jesuit movement had not covered a political menace. He guaranteed the privileges of the monasteries, restored and insured their revenues, and granted funds for the publication of religious works. He even enforced ecclesiastical jurisdiction, and punished by the pillory and banishment all those who broke the monastic vows. But at the same time he debarred the priesthood from any pai'ticipation in the government. He abolished the custom of employing Buddhist agents in diplomatic amenities with Korea, and appointed a lay officer to control all affairs connected with the clergy. The influence of Buddhism was on the wane. Under the protection afforded to the monldiood, and the cultured ease they enjoyed, the monasteries became universities whose occupants were famed more for their erudition than for their hoHness. The single new sect which originated in that era differed from the others only in discipline, a subject widely discussed in that age of order and strict regime.

Like Buddhism, Confucianism had in its later developments become super-social and indifferent to politics through its absorption of Taoist and Buddhist ideals. In China, from the latter part of the Tang dynasty, Confucianism tended to become religious instead of, being purely ethical, as in previous days. In Japan this tendency was even more pronounced, for during our feudal age all branches of learning •-^ were confined to the Buddhists, so that ~ x-^-^he early teachers in the Tokugawa

academies were mostly monks who had been induced to return to a secular life in order to impart secular teaching. They did not give up their Buddhist costume for a long time, and used to shave their heads even after they began to wear swords like other samurai. They were all followers of the school of Shiuki, a Neo-Confucian of the Sung dynasty, and the teaching they imparted accorded well with their dress. Neo-Confucianism, a product of that remarkable age of "illumination," so rich in creative efforts both in art and literature, aimed at a synthesis of Taoist, Buddhist, and Confucian thought, and marks the result of a brilliant effort to mirror the whole of Asiatic consciousness. Its exponents differed in their interpretation of the Confucian classic, according to their mental affini-^

ties with Chinese or Indian thought. Some of them were called " strayed Zen," in the same sense as Sanchara-charya, the Xeo-Brahmanist, was accused of being a " disguised Buddhist." Shiuki, however, through his greater leaning toward the doctrines of the Chinese sage, was recognized as the central figure of Xeo-Confucianism. His Commentaries on Confucius were made official text-books by the Emperor Yan-lu of the jNIing djmasty, and his school was accepted as orthodox by lyeyasu. The general trend of Xeo-Confucianism, even wath Shiuki, tended to make it abstract and speculative, so that as a result its votaries differed but slightly from the followers of Buddha, making self-concentration an important part of mental exercise. The]Ming scholars, with their formal-

istic instincts, dogmatized the instinic-tions of Shiuki, and wasted their energy on his abstract rules of morahty and terminology,—an example followed by the Japanese academicians. Confucianism was thus deprived of its very essence—practical ethics. " As foolish as a scholar," was a common witticism of Tokugawa days. Two schools of heresy tried to stem the tide and infuse vitality into the Confucian doctrines, but they commanded an insignificant minority, for the Tokugawa censorship was rigorous in suppressing all schools of thought that dared to differ from the orthodox teaching of its own academy.

Thus the knowledge that lyeyasu
imparted to the nation was, after all,
of a kind that gave no great stimulus
to social activity. His system of in-

struction formed as much a part of his scheme for preserving absolutism as any of the military precautions he took against the power of the Kioto court or that of the daimiates. Yet it is but fair to say that the encouragement of learning inaugurated by him had much to do with the formation of modern Japanese character. Buddhism and Xeo-Confucianism (which is truly Buddhist in its nature) gave to the nation that meditative trend of mind which makes it possible for it to face emergencies ^^ath calmness. If he did not initiate an era of progress, at least he taught stability. If it had not been for this, the fierce turmoil of the Restoration, with its violent accession of Western thought, would have swept Japan from her ancient anchorage into an unknown and stormy sea.

BUDDHISM AND CONFUCIANISM

Asia is nothing if not spiritual, but the man of the spirit is not one of names or forms. He comes, we wist not whence, and, Hke another Lohengrin, vanishes when revealed, to follow the quest mysterious in regions unknown. True spirituality forsook the luxury of the monastery and the ease of the academy, to take its rugged seat in the breast of the lonely ronin-scholar. Like the snow-covered narcissus pining for a glimpse of heaven, its silent soul bore the quenchless prophecy of spring.

THE VOICE FROM WITHIN

IT seems to be the general impression among foreigners that it was the West who, with the touch of a magic wand, suddenly roused us from the sleep of centuries. The real cause of our awakening, however, came from within. Our national consciousness had already begun to stir when, in the year 1853, Commodore Perry reached our shores, and had waited but for that event to inaugurate a universal movement toward renationalization.

Three separate schools of thought united to cause the regeneration of Japan. The first taught her to inquire;

THE VOICE FROM WITHIN

the second, to act; the third, for what to act. All were tiny streams at their outset, finding their source in the solitary souls of independent thinkers who nursed them always under censure, often in banishment. They even coursed from within the prison walls and trickled from the scaffold. They were almost hidden beneath the rank vegetation of conventionalism until the moment when they united to leap in cataracts of patriotic zeal inundating the whole nation.

The first, known as the Kogaku (School of Classic Learning), arose at the end of the seventeenth century as a protest against the dogmas of the governmental academies. Its originators claimed that the Neo-Confucianism of Shiuki as taught in the academies was not really Confucianism, but a new-

THE AWAKENING OF JAPAN

f angled interpretation of Buddhism and Taoism. They invited scholars to return to the original texts of the sage himself and find anew the real meaning thereof. It was a bold stand for them to take, considering that Shiuki's commentaries were considered orthodox and their authority had remained unquestioned both in China and Japan since the Sung Illumination of the eleventh century. This school for the first time frees the Toku-gawa mind from the trammels of for malism, though its liberalism does not result in any particular conclusions."" Its very attitude, that of inquiry, prevents it from crystallizing into any single solution of Confucianism. Some of its adherents, like Sorai, go as far as to maintain that Confucius was purely a political philosopher and not a teacher of ethics. Some, on the other hand, like

THE VOICE FROM WITHIN

Yamaga-Soko, to whom we owe the development of the Samurai Code on a Confucian basis, found in Japanese institutions the expression of the moral law of the Chinese sage. Yet however they differed individually in their conclusions, they united in being heretical toward the orthodox Tokugawa notions, and all were objects of disapprobation to the authorities,—Yamaga-Soko, who commanded a considerable following, being banished from Yedo to the distant and insignificant daimiate of Akho. Yet even during his confinement there his personality inspired the well-known Forty-seven Ronins to attempt their memorable feat of loyalty, remarkable not only as revealing a new ideal of samurai-hood, but eloquent in its silent protest against the Tokugawa regime.

The second school, which started at nearly the same time as the first, is called the School of Oyomei, from the Japanese pronunciation of Wangyang-ming, the name of its founder. This remarkable man was a great general as well as scholar who Hved in China at the beginning of the sixteenth century, under the Ming djmasty. He never ceased to discourse even during the brilliant campaigns in which he was victorious over the rebels in Southern China. His philosophy was an advance on the Neo-Confucianism of Shiuki, whose doctrines, however, he accepted in the main. His principal contribution lay in his definition of knowledge. With him all knowledge was useless unless expressed in action. To know was to be. Virtue was real in so far only as it was manifested in '■ -74.

deeds. The whole universe was incessantly surging on to higher spheres of development, calling upon all to join in its glorious advance. To realize their teachings it was necessary to live the life of the sages themselves, to consecrate one's whole energy to the service of mankind. Thus he brought Confucianism again into its true domain, that ^ of practical ethics.

His doctrines appear to have had only a temporary influence on China itself, but they possessed a peculiar charm for the Japanese mind, and later furnished one of the principal incentives toward the accomplishment of the Restoration. One of the pioneers of this school in Japan has produced such an impression on the moral life of the districts around Lake Biwa that his memory is still cherished as that of the

y

"Living Confucius." Another, devoting himself to the material vv^elfare of the people, has left in his engineering feats for the irrigation of the Okayama provinces a monument to the zeal inspired by Oyomei; yet he had to suffer for heresy and died in exile and disgrace.

The Oyomian scholars of Japan went further than the Chinese in their dynamic conception of the cosmic force. Their predilection for Indian modes of thought, especially for that of the Zen sect of Buddhism, made them lay great stress on the idea of change, with the result that they came to conclusions curiously akin to many of those held by modern evolutionists. The Buddhas of the past were not the Bud-dhas of the future, for they must include the former and something more.

Every new life was built on the debris of the past and amid the tumultuous crash of a myriad of dissolving worlds. A reincarnation was self-realization on a different plane. How magnificent is change! How beautiful the great transition known as life and death!

The Japanese Oyomians delighted in the image of the dragon. Have you seen the dragon? Approach him cautiously, for no mortal can survive the sight of his entire body. The Eastern dragon is not the gruesome monster of medieval imagination, but the genius of strength and goodness. He is the spirit of change, therefore of life itself. We associate him with the supreme power or that sovereign cause which pervades everything, taking new forms according to its surroundings, yet never seen in a final shape. The

dragon is the great mystery itself. Hidden in the caverns of inaccessible mountains, or coiled in the unfathomed depth of the sea, he awaits the time when he slowly rouses himself into activity. He unfolds himself in the storm clouds; he w^ashes his mane in the blackness of the seething whirlpools. His claws are in the fork of the lightning, his scales begin to glisten in the bark of rain-swept j3ine-trees. His voice is heard in the hurricane which, scattering the withered leaves of the forest, quickens a new spring. The dragon reveals himself only to vanish. He is a glorious symbolic image of that elasticity of organism which shakes off the inert mass of exhausted matter. Coiling again and again on his strength, he sheds his crusted skin amid the battle of elements, and for an instant stands half

revealed by the brilliant shininier of his scales. He strikes not till his throat is touched. Then woe to him who dallies with the terrible one!

The dragon is said never to be the same. What flower is? What life? The secret of knowledge, according to the Oyomians, was to penetrate behind the mask which change imposed upon things. So-called facts and forms were merely incidents beneath which the real life lay hidden. This they loved to illustrate by the Taoist parable of the Real Horse. Once upon a time, it is related, a king of China was desirous of procuring the best horse in the world, wherefore he asked Hakuraku, all-knowing in horses, to make search far and wide. After a long time Hakuraku retin-ned and reported to the king that a bay mare on a certain pas-

ture was the most perfect horse existent. Thereupon the king sent vassals laden with treasures to bring the steed to his court. When, however, they came to the place described by Hakuraku they found not a bay mare, but a black stallion. This they brought back with them, and it was found to be the paragon of equine beauty and strength. To the true connoisseur of horses the real horse was visible in something beyond the secondary features of color and sex. Even thus it is with all true knowledge, said the Oyomians.

The orthodox academicians were doubly hostile to the Oyomei School as a perversion of their own Neo-Confu-cianism. The terror of their censorship lay not so much in open attacks on the doctrines themselves as in the treacherous and unexpected manner in which

they brought punishment upon their holders.

Yet, in spite of this, the new idea was fostered and slowly gained ground in those distant daimiates where censorial interference was comparatively slight. It is significant that the two provinces of Satsuma and Choshiu, from which all the great statesmen of modern Japan come, were the chief refuge of this school of philosophy. Among those of our generals and admirals who have distinguished themselves in the Chinese and Russian wars, many were brought up as youths in the principles of Oyo-mei. This it is which makes them calm amid danger, resourcefid in planning, and ever alert to meet the dictates of change. It was largely due to the ^ipread of Oyomian philosophy that Japan recognized the dragon amid the

boiling ferment of the Restoration. Like the Real Horse of Hakuraku, the spirit of Old Japan, in spite of the accretions of centuries, was still manifest. The Tokugawa authorities had everything to fear from the revolutionary nature of the Oyomei doctrine, whose followers hesitated at nothing where their idea of righteousness was concerned. It was Oshiwo, a celebrated Oyomei scholar of Osaka, who with all his disciples rose in open revolt when the governor of that city refused for some insufficient reason to grant subsistence to the populace during the severe famine of 1837. He fired on the garrison and held them in check while he distributed the contents of the government granaries to the famished people, after which he calmly met his death. His mental attitude may be well seen where, in an interesting philosophical work, he says: "Strike like the lightning, be terrible like the thunder, but remember that the sky itself is always clear above."

Neither the heresy of the Classic School nor the virility of the Oyo-mei School would in themselves have evolved the political conception that led to the Restoration. They were, after all, but differentiations in Confucianism, and Confucianism ordained obedience to existing authority provided that the moral life of the community was not thereby destroyed. Hence it was that the Ming scholars offered no resistance to the Manchu rule. It was for this same reason that the Tokugawa Confucians, whatever their school, never dreamed of instituting a change in our political system. Oyomei taught to act, but not for what or for whom. This deficiency it was the mission of the Historical School to supply.

The Historical School was not a heresy and was therefore rarely regarded with suspicion by the censors. On the contrary, the Tokugawas themselves encouraged it, for it accorded with their traditional policy. The movement began early in their rule with a compilation of the genealogies of the chief families in the empire and the publication of histories redounding to the credit of the Tokugawas themselves. One important history written by the chief academician of his time is interesting as evincing the utmost servility to Confucian classicism, in that the author tries to prove the descent of the Mikado from the Chinese sages. By the beginning of the eighteenth century however, the pure light of research appeared in the study of philology. This movement, led by Keichiu-acharya and culminating in the illustrious works of Motoori and Harumi, opened up in our ancient poetry and history a new vista of thought. Toward the end of the century the study of archaeology increased to such an extent that the Toku-gawa government and wealthy daimios vied with each other in the collection of rare manuscripts and encyclopedic publications on art, while well-known connoisseurs were appointed to investigate and record the treasures of the old monasteries at Nara and Kioto. All this continued to lift the veil which had hung for so many centuries over the past. This was indeed the era of Renaissance in Japan.

The acquisition of historical knowledge resulted in the revivification of Shintoism. The purity of this ancient cult had been overflowed by successive waves of continental influence until it had almost entirely lost its original character. In the ninth century it became merely a branch of esoteric Buddhism and delighted in mystic symbolism, while after the fifteenth century it was entirely Neo-Confucian in spirit and accepted the cosmic interpretation of the Taoists. But with the revival of ancient learning it became divested of these alien elements. Shintoism as formulated in the beginning of the nineteenth century is a religion of ancestrism —a worship of pristine purity handed down from the age of the gods. It teaches adherence to those ancestral ideals of the Japanese race, simplicity and honesty, obedience to the ancestral rule vested in the person of the Mikado, and devotion to the ancestral land on whose consecrated and divine shores no foreign conqueror has ever set his foot. It called upon Japan to break loose from blind slavery to Chinese and In-dian ideals, and to rely upon herself.

The historic spirit swept on through the realms of literature, art, and religion, until it finally reached the heart of the samurai. Till then its effects had been brilliant but not momentous, its expressions scholar^ and therefore limited in scope. A democratization of the new message is found in the works of the early writers of the last century, among whom the poet-historian Rai-Sanyo stands foremost in rank. It was from his lucid pages that the full meaning of the past dawned on the minds of the young samurai and ronins. Their memories traveled back to the days when the imperial sanctity was forgotten and the chrj^santhemum cowered before the cruel blast of Ashikaga arrogance, while even the palace itself, with none so loyal as to undertake its repair, was sinking in ruin within sight of the Golden Pavilion of the shoguns. Sadly they read the poems of some lonely loyalist who, like a solitary cuckoo, poured his sad song into the moonless night.

They dwelt with mingled pride and sorrow on the story of the Emperor Go-daigo, who broke the power of the Ka-makura shogunate and for a time reestablished legitimate rule. They thought of his undaunted courage in raising the country against the usurpers, of his exile to the distant island of Sado, of his miraculous escape in a fishing-boat, of his triumphs over the enemy, and of his fastness in the mountain of Yoshino,^ where he held his court until the time when the cherry-blossoms covered his mausoleum with their tribute of tender homage.

The gaunt image of IMasashige rose before them, that hero who fought for the Emperor Godaigo knowing that his cause was already lost. They read how he it was who first dared answer the imperial summons to fight the usurper, how he planned and carried out the guerrilla warfare which led to a temporary restitution of the Mikado's power, and claimed no reward when his work was accomplished. " What is thy' last wish?" said he to his brother as, wounded unto death, they both emerged

^ Yoshino, a hill in the Nara prefecture noted from ancient times for its cherry-blossoms.

from their last terrible battle with the Ashikaga hosts. Smiling, he listened to the swift reply, " I wish to be born again to strike a blow for the Mikado," and said, " Though Buddhists teach that such wishes are sinful and lead to the hell of Asuras, yet not for once only but for seven lives do I wish to be reborn for that same end " ; then each fell by the other's sword. They read how Masatsura, the son of Mashashige, refused the first beauty of the court, who was deeply attached to him, when the Mikado offered her to him as a reward for his hereditary loyalty, pleading that his life was for death and not love.

Soon as the memory of past ages came over the samurai, the lost glory of the Son of Heaven flashed upon them. They saw the Mikado himself leading his army to victory. They heard their ancestors beating their shields with their swords, as they sang the war-song of Otomo, the terrible joy of dying by the Mikado's side. They wept when they thought of the shadow that had come over the throne. They made pilgrimages to the imperial mausoleums, which had long been left to decay, and washed their moss-covered steps with tears. Who w^ere the Toku-gawas who dared to stand between them and their legitimate sovereign? Oh, to die—to die for the Mikado!

The historic spirit now stood sword in hand, and the sword was one of no mean steel. The samurai, like his weapon, was cold, but never forgot the fire in which he was forged. His impetuosity was always tempered by his code of honor. In the feudal days Zen had taught him self-restraint and made courteousness the mark of bravery. Confucianism had in the Toku-gawa period intensified that sense of duty which made him disregard all obstacles. He did not court useless danger, for his courage was never questioned. He marched to certain death not with the blind fury of fanaticism but with a set resolution of doing whatever was demanded of him. The historical spirit in penetrating his soul made him a new being. All the devotion which had formerly been consecrated to the service of his immediate liege was now laid at the feet of the Mikado.

Soon the historical spirit began to permeate the ranks of the daimios. It first entered the souls of those Tozama daimios who, like the lords of Satsuma and Choshiu, felt a hereditary animosity to the shogunate. Later on it began to influence even the princes of the Toku-gawa family, especially the princes of Mito and the lords of Echizen. The scholars of these daimiates, with their Shinto and Oyomian tendencies, were the apostles of the Restoration. It is to be noted that Keiki, last of the sho-guns, who voluntarily gave up the reins of government to the Mikado, was a prince of Mito.

The hour had come when dreams were to be translated into action, and the sword was to leave the quiet of the scabbard and leap forth with the fury of lightning.

Strange whispers traveled from the cities to the villages. The lotus trembled above the turbid waters, the stars began to pale before the dawn, and that mighty hush which bespeaks the coming storm fell on the nation. Oyomei was abroad and the dragon was calling forth the hurricane. It was at this moment that the West appeared on our horizon.

THE WHITE DISASTER

TO MOST Eastern nations the advent of the West has been by no means an unmixed blessing. Thinking to welcome the benefits of increased commerce, they have become the victims of foreign imperialism; believing in the philanthropic aims of Christian missionaries, they have bowed before the messengers of military aggression. For them the earth is no longer filled with that peace which pillowed their contentment. If the guilty conscience of some European nations has conjured up the specter of a Yellow Peril, may not the suffering soul of Asia wail over the realities of the White Disaster.

To the mind of the average Westerner it may seem but natural to regard with feelings of unmingled triumph that world of to-day in which organization has made of society a huge machine ministering to its own necessities. It is the rapid development of mechanical invention which has created the present era of locomotion and speculation, a development which is working itself out into various expressions, as commercialism and industrialism, accompanied by a tendency toward the universal occidentalization of etiquette and language. This movement, resulting in a rapid expansion of wealth and prestige, originated in a profound realization of the glory of manhood, of comradeship, and of mutual trust. The restlessness that constantly moves its home from the steamer to the hotel, from the railway station to the bathing resort, has brought about the possibility of a cosmopolitan culture. The nineteenth century has witnessed a wonderful spread in the blessings of scientific sanitation and surgery. Knowledge as well as finance has become organized, and large communities are made capable of collective action and the development of a single personal consciousness. To the inhabitant of the West all this may well be food for satisfaction; to him it may seem inconceivable that others should think differently. Yet to the bland irony of China the machine appears as a toy, not an ideal. The venerable East still distinguishes between means and ends. The West is for progress, but progress toward what? When material efficiency is complete, what end, asks Asia, will have been ac-

complished? When the passion of fraternity has culminated in universal cooperation, what purpose is it to serve? If mere self-interest, where do we find the boasted advance?

The picture of Western glory unfortunately has a reverse. Size alone does not constitute true greatness, and the enjoyment of luxury does not always result in refinement. The individuals who go to the making up of the great machine of so-called modern civilization become the slaves of mechanical habit and are ruthlessly dominated by the monster they have created. In spite of the vaunted freedom of the West, true individuality is destroyed in the competition for wealth, and happiness and contentment are sacrificed to an incessant craving for more. The West takes pride in its emancipation from

medieval superstition, but what of that idolatrous worship of wealth that has taken its place? What sufferings and discontent lie hidden behind the gorgeous mask of the present? The voice of socialism is a wail over the agonies of Western economics,—the tragedy of Capital and Labor.

But with a hunger unsatisfied by its myriad victims in its own broad lands, the West also seeks to prey upon the East. The advance of Europe in Asia means not merely the imposition of social ideals which the East holds to be crude if not barbarous, but also the subversion of all existing law and authority. The Western ships which brought their civilization also brought conquests, protectorates, ex-territorial jurisdiction, spheres of influence, and what not of debasement, till the name of the Oriental

has become a synonym for the degenerate, and the word " native " an epithet for slaves.

In Japan the race of those fiery patriots who fifty years ago shouted, "Away with the Western barbarians!" with all the lusty enthusiasm of the Chinese Boxers, is entirely gone. The tremendous change which has since me over our political life, and the ma-rial advantages we have gained by foreign contact, have so completely revolutionized national sentiment in regard to the West that it has become almost impossible for us to conceive what it was that so aroused the antagonism of our grandfathers. On the contrary, we have become so eager to identify ourselves with European civilization instead of Asiatic that our continental neighbors regard us as renegades—nay,

even as an embodiment of the White Disaster itself. But our mental standpoint of a few generations back was that of the conservative Chinese patriot of to-day, and we saw in Western advance but the probable encompassing of our ruin. To the down-trodden Oriental the glory of

Europe is but the humiliation of Asia.

If we place ourselves in the position of a Chinese patriot of to-day we shall be able to understand how the march of contemporary events appeared to our grandfathers. Their fears were not altogether without reason, for to the wounded imagination of Orientals history will tell of the gradual advance of the White Disaster which was descending on Asia. The Italian Renaissance marks the time when, freed from its chains, the roving spirit of Western enterprise first began to seize upon any corner of the globe where was aught to be gained. When Marco Polo returned from the Chinese court, he bore tidings of the untold treasures of the extreme Orient. America was merely an accidental discovery on the part of Spain in her attempt to reach the coveted wealth of India. We can recall those days of Portuguese cruelty and Dutch treachery, when the cow's hide gained a colony and the concession for a factory resulted in the establishment of an empire.

The beginning of the seventeenth century shows the rise of the East India companies of the French, Dutch, Danish, and English, the gratification of whose political ambitions, however, remained as yet unsatisfied owing to the struggles of mutual rivalry, the solidity of the Mussulman power of Delhi, and their awe of that great Turkish empire which still bravely bore the brunt of Western advance and often hurled it back to the walls of Vienna. But the brightness of the Crescent was fast waning before the combined persistence of the West, and soon the disastrous treaty of Kutchuk-Kainarji inaugurated the imposition of Russian interference in the affairs of the Porte. In 1803 the last of the Grand Moguls became a British pensioner. In 1839, Abdul Medjid ascended the throne of Osmanli under the "protection" of European powers.

With the increase in credit and capital during the latter half of the eighteenth century, the inventive energy of European industrialism is set in motion. Coal takes the place of wood in smelting, and the flying shuttle, the spinning-jenny, the mule, the power-loom, and the steam-engine all spring up in formidable array. Commercialism makes the very life of the West depend upon her finding markets for her goods. Her role is now to sell, and that of the East to buy. War is declared from her factories, and the protests of her more humane statesmen are drowned in the noise of thundering mills. What chance has individualized Eastern trade against the sweeping batteries of organized commerce? Cheapness and competition, like the mitrailleuse, under whose cover they advance, now sweep away the crafts. The economic life of the Orient, founded on land and labor and deprived of a protective tariff through high-handed diplomatic action, succumbs to the army of the machine and capital.

What has become of India? It is today a country where the names of Asoka and Vikramaditya are even forgotten. It is a country of rajas whose breasts are starry with dishonor, and of national congresses that dare not protest. Burma was in existence but yesterday: in the rubies of Thebaw cries the innocent blood of Mandalay. The Kohi-noor is even as a teardrop of Golconda. What need to mention the painful comedies enacted in Persia and Siam or to call attention to the "protectorate" established by France over Tonkin? Protectorate! Against whom?

In 1842 a Christian nation forces opium on China at the mouth of the cannon and extorts Hongkong. In 1860, on a slight pretext, the joint armies of France and England invade Pekin and sack the Summer Palace, whose treasures are now the pride of the European museums, while the Russians always maintain a steady encroachment upon the hereditary domains of the Celestial Empire along the borders of the Amur and Hi. The kindly intervention of the Triple Coalition after the Japanese war was but a farce, for thereby Russia gained Port Arthur, Germany Kiau-chau, and France a tighter grasp on Yunnan. It is true that the defilement of their sacred shrines goaded the Boxers to a passionate outburst of fury; but what could their old-fashioned arms avail against the combined armies of the allied powers? Their ill-judged efforts only resulted in the heaping of indignities upon China and the payment by her of exorbitant indemnities. In spite of repeated promises of evacuation, Russia has endeavored to establish herself permanently in Manchuria, and the persecuted inhabitants of that province behold the graveyards of their beloved forefathers turned into railway stations, while Cossack horses find stabling in the sacred Temple of Heaven. If Asia was old-fashioned, was Europe just? If China tried to lift her head, if the worm turned in its agony, did not Europe at once raise the cry of the Yellow Peril? Veriljs the glory of the'i West is the humiliation of Asia.

To Japan the armed embassy of the United States of America in 1853 seemed a dread image of that White Disaster whose advent had proved so fatal to other Eastern countries. Eleven years before that event tlie Opium War in China had exposed the unscrupulous nature of Western aggression. The Dutch, who kept us informed of the European encroachment on Asia, did not hesitate to enhance the value of their friendship by painting the deeds of other Western nations in the darkest colors. In fact, unfortunately, we had already had some experience of foreign rapacity in the Russian advance from the north.

It is a curious coincidence that the first European nation—and let us hope it may be the last—whom we have met in battle array is the power whose acts first warned us of the possibility of foreign complications. Russia, sweeping down from Siberia and Kamchatka, long ago laid her hands upon our territory of Sakhalin and the Kurile Islands. In the end of the eighteenth century the Russians committed ravages in Yezo itself, and in 1806 the Tokugawas had to place a military governor in Hako-date to guard against their further depredations. Alarming stories of Northern encroachments were poured into our excited ears, and many daimios offered by themselves to chase back the intruders. In 1830 Naraiki of Mito, a powerful prince of the Tokugawa family, proposed to settle in Yezo with all his retainers and the entire population of his daimiate. He melted all the bronze bells of the temples in his territory, casting a number of immense cannon, and drilled his samurai in preparation for an emergency. His zeal was, however, misconstrued by the Tokugawa government and he was obliged to abdicate in favor of his son and remain in retirement. RussojDhobes were imprisoned for spreading false alarms, and many died in confinement. It is interesting to find among some of their memoirs prophecies of Russian aggrandizement in Asia which have been but too truly fulfilled.

The aj)pearance of American warships in the bay of Yedo was a mighty shock. Hitherto the alarms of foreign attack had meant but little to the country at large, for it was a long cry to

Hakodate or Nagasaki; but now within a day's march of the city of Yedo lay the black hulks of a formidable fleet whose admiral refused to retire until a treaty was signed. Recollection of the Tartar armada flashed through the minds of our grandfathers. Was the samurai to be intimidated in his own waters? Was not the divine land always prepared to repel an invasion? What right had a foreign nation to impose a commerce which we did not want, a friendship which we did not ask? To

THE WHITE DISASTER

arms! J hoi! J hoi! Away with the barbarians! The alarm-bells clanged throughout the country. Foam-covered riders rushed through every castle gate, spreading the momentous news. Spears were torn from their racks and ancient armor was eagerly dragged from dust-covered caskets. Night and day could be heard the clanging of steel on anvils forging the accoutrements of war. The old prince of]Mito was summoned from his hermitage to take command, and his cannon lined the principal points of defense. Buddhists wore away their rosaries in invoking Kartikiya, the war-god, and Shinto priests fasted while they called on the sea and the tempest to destroy the invader.

The historic spirit that had been smoldering in our national consciousness only waited for this moment to

THE AWAKENING OF JAPAN

burst forth in a fiery expression of unity. Custom and formalism were alike forgotten in this hour of common danger, and for the first time in two hundred years the daimios were asked by the Tokugawa government to deliberate over a matter of state. For the first time in seven centuries the Shogun sent a special envoy to the Mikado to consult about the policj^ of the empire, and for the first time in the history of our nation, the high and the low alike were invited to oiFer suggestions as to what steps should be taken for the protection of the ancestral land. We became one, and the Night of Asia fled forever before the rays of the Rising Sun.

THE CABINET AND THE BOUDOIR

HAD it not been for the timely arrival of the American Embassy and the determined attitude which it took in regard to Japan's relations with the outside world, we might have entered upon an era of internal discord culminating in a civil war far worse than anything that preceded the Restoration of 18G8. The immediate effect of the arrival of the American Embassy was to reconsolidate the fast-wanino-power of the Tokugawa governmeut. Putting in abeyance all minor matters of dispute, the entire nation looked to '

THE AWAKENING OF JAPAN

the Shogun, as the representative of all existing authority, to lead the forces of Japan against what was regarded as a Western invasion. Thus the Toku-gawa government was given a new lease of life and its final overthrow postponed for fifteen years, during which time ultra-reformists were kept from running riot and the nation was given a chance to prepare itself for the momentous change which was to come. Had the Tokugawas better understood their own position, they might under this new condition of affairs, have retained their power for an indefinite period of time; but, unfortunately for them, there developed out of the rivalry between the cabinet and the boudoir an element of discord which brought about the ultimate downfall of the entire Tokugawa system.

CABINET AND BOUDOIR

Like all Eastern monarchies, the To-kugawa shogunate led a twofold existence, that of the outer ministry and that of the inner household. Of these two modes of expression, the former exhibits the sovereign as one who represents the united political wisdom of the country handed down through a long succession of experiences, the latter as an autocrat whose will is law. The ideal ruler, who stopped in the midst of a banquet to listen to the grievances of his people and preferred the discourse of sour-visaged councilors to the sweet music of the court beauties, confined himself exclusively to the first role. But even in Confucian lands human nature is weak. The fortunes of a dynasty have often fluctuated with the adherence of its representative to one or the other of these policies; and it is a signifi- cant fact that in Chinese history we find the preponderance of the household influence always resulting in rebellion, whereas that of the cabinet is overthrown only by the aggression of some foreign power. In more recent days a sort of compromise has generally been effected between these influences, virtually creating a twofold expression of the sovereign will. This arrangement has occasioned many awkward complications, especially where diplomatic relations with foreign nations have been concerned: the household may deny what the cabinet has afiirmed, and vice versa.

The power of the Chinese imperial household, to whose deliberations, according to Celestial customs, no male was admitted, was often wielded by the Empress or some lady politician who from her boudoir pulled the reins of the government to the dismay of cabinet ministers. Some of these women were possessed of remarkable genius and succeeded in assuming entire control of the state. Empress Lo of the Hang and Empress Wu of the Tang dynasty are well-known examples of the usurpation of full sovereignty by a woman. The present Empress Dowager of China affords a remarkable instance of the ascendancy which the household may possess over the Tsung-li-yamen, or cabinet.

Under the Tokugawa shogunate there was constant friction between the cabinet and the boudoir. The ministers, chosen from among the ablest representatives of those daimiates which had been created by the Tokugawas, strove to mfiintain the hereditary policy of Iyeyasu, which had in their eyes almost the authority of a national constitution. They were for the most part astute statesmen who thoroughly understood the spirit of the nation, and never, in spite of their absolutism, outraged the feelings of the public. It was owing to their influence that the Sho-gun, even if personally of weak character, generally commanded the respect of his subjects. When, however, the Shogun fell under the influence of the boudoir, he became the hated despot who, regardless of public opinion, passed measures inimical to the national welfare. Unfortunately, in these cases the cabinet made but slight protest, for the code of the samurai forbade resistance to the will of the overlord.

The ladies of Yedo Castle had been active participators in the Tokugawa rule even in the time of Iyeyasu, who found among them many trusted friends and able councilors. It formed a part of his system to send them on secret and delicate missions, and they had come to be a well-recognized power in the government of his successors. In the case of a shogun at all inclined to be autocratic, the ladies surrounding his private life exerted an immense influence. Either in the person of his mother, his wife, his nurse, or his favorite, they so constantly influenced his feelings and sought to mold his actions that he needed to be a man of very strong character to remain untram-meled by these silken bonds. They possessed a hereditary policy of their own, which, based on woman's instinct of conservatism and hatred of compromise, was the dread of all cabinet ministers who attempted reforms. Their interference was not like the temporary meddling of a Madame Pompadour or a Duchesse de Montespan, but that of a whole line of female cardinals. It was owing to the antagonism of the boudoir that the Tokugawa statesman Rakuwo failed to accomplish his proposed reorganization of local government. It was through their influence that Mid-zuno-Echizen was prevented from enforcing his sumptuary laws, which aimed at the correction of many existent abuses. During the closing years of the Tokugawa government many wise measures proposed by the cabinet met with defeat owing to the ascendancy in power of the boudoir.

At the time of the first American Embassy, the reigning Shogun, twelfth of his line, was a young and weak prince who had, however, in the person of Abe-Isenokami, an able prime minister who showed a remarkable grasp of the situation and inaugurated that enlightened policy to which Japan owes her present position. The real significance of his acts has been quite obscured beneath a mass of conflicting criticism and the ignominy which attaches to the statesmen of a fallen dynasty. Even his negotiation of a treaty of amity with Commodore Perry in the face of a dissenting majority has been minimized by his detractors, yet it was this treaty which first brought us in touch with the rest of the world. His moderation was not cowardice; if he had allowed himself to be carried away by the belligerent spirit which animated the daimios, Japan might have made a pitiful exhibition of herself. A refusal to treat with the Embassy would probably have resulted in a bombardment, and in spite of the fiery bravery of the samurai, what would their old-fashioned cannon and fortifications have availed against the well-equipped Americans? It is due to the full recognition by Abe-Isenokami of our unpreparedness for war that Japan was saved from any such disaster. Our sincere thanks are also due to the American admiral, who showed infinite patience and fairness in his negotiations. Oriental nations never forget a kindness, and international kindnesses are unfortunately extremely rare. The name of Commodore Perry has become so dear to us that, on the fiftieth anniversary of his arrival, the people erected a monument at the spot where he landed.

It is not to be supposed that Abe-Isenokami realized the full importance of foreign intercourse, or even welcomed it. Like other men of his time, he merely considered it as a necessary evil. His knowledge of the West was but scanty, and he left the burden of treating with the Americans to his minister of foreign affairs, Hotta-Bitchiunokami, who later succeeded to the premiership after the death of Abe. He recognized nevertheless how necessary it was for Japan to acquire Western knowledge, so that she might be able to defend herself against foreign invasion. This he was at length able to impress upon the Tokugawa authorities, and the warlike daimios were prevailed upon to keep quiet during his lifetime. He opened, under government patronage, a school in which various branches of foreign science were for the first time openly taught: the present Imperial University of Tokio is a development from this school. Hitherto the pursuit of foreign knowledge except that of medicine had been interdicted, and students had been obliged to do their work in secret and under great difficulties. Now, however, any one who proved himself worthy was promoted and encouraged in his work, while our soldiers were trained in the Dutch and French systems of drill. Both war-ships and merchant vessels were ordered from Holland, and young samurai were sent to study their construction and management; this was the beginning of the present Japanese navy. The prohibition against building ships beyond a certain size was revoked, and many daimios, like those of Mito and Satsuma, vied in constructing them.

CABINET AND BOUDOIR

The main idea of Abe-Isenokami seemed to have been to consolidate the Tokugawa rule on a new basis. He appears to have appreciated the fact that a great change had come over the nation, and that the fast-decaying prestige of the Tokugawa government could be saved from complete destruction only by the assimilation of new energy. It was his intention to make the shogunate the center of all the forces that moved the empire. It was with this idea that he initiated the custom of approaching the Mikado and the assembh^ of daimios on all questions of state: a great mistake in the eyes of Tokugawa historians. He strengthened the allegiance of the lord of Satsuma, most powerful of the daimios, by bringing about the marriage of his daughter to the Sho-gun. He kept the old prince of Mito

THE AWAKENING OF JAPAN

in good humor by making active preparations for war. He corrected many existing abuses, instituted reforms in administration, appointed able men even from the lower ranks of the samurai to responsible positions, and did all he could for the revival of Tokugawa prestige.

Next to the foreign question the most vital problem of the day was as to who should succeed to the shogunate on the death of the present incumbent, a childless and confirmed invalid. Indeed, this latter question proved itself perhaps the more important of the two, for the ultimate downfall of the Tokugawas resulted from the manner in which it was finally settled. Among the Tokugawa princes Keiki, the fourth son of the old prince of Mito, seemed the most suitable candidate for the succession.

CABINET AND BOUDOIR

He was adored by the daimios and samurai, not onl\'7d^ on account of his father, but for his own fine personality and ability. His devotion to the Mikado was well known, and it was said that the court of Kioto would be pleased to have him as shogun. Abe saw in Keiki's succession a great possibility for solidifying the Tokugawa rule, as an able shogun backed by the daimios and the Kioto court, might accomplish almost anything. There was but one difficulty in the way of his appointment, and that was that the present Shogun and the ladies of his court disliked him. As a samurai and vassal, Abe's preeminent duty was to obey the wishes of his master, while as a minister he recognized the power of the ladies of Yedo Castle. He knew that to the conservative policy of the bou-

THE AWAKENING OF JAPAN

doir his various innovations were distasteful in the extreme, and that it feared the appointment of a strong-minded shogun, such as Keiki promised to be, who might refuse to become a mere puppet in its hands. On this account Abe dared not show his hand, for he was aware of the great power which the boudoir could bring to bear upon the cabinet to overthrow all its efforts toward a reorganization of the Toku-gawa rule. His attitude toward the problem of succession was so cautious as to appear almost indecisive. Had he been spared a few years longer, he might have accomplished his object; but in 1857 he succumbed to a short illness and died at the age of thirty-nine. Thus perished the last great statesman who might have retrieved the sinking fortunes of the Tokugawas.

CABINET AND BOUDOIR

Hotta-Bitchiunokami, who succeeded Abe as prime minister, although he did not possess the same abihty, tried to follow out the policy of his predecessor. He did not command the respect of the Kioto court and unwittingly alienated the affections of the daimios. He was almost without supporters by the time he left Yedo, in the spring of 1858, to obtain the imperial ratification to the new treaty whose terms had been drawn up by him and the American consul, Townsend Harris. Times were indeed changed when a Tokugawa prime minister was obliged to go in person to Kioto to answer the queries of those court nobles who had formerlj^ trembled in his presence. But the Kioto court had already tasted power and would fain drink to the full. To the members of the imperial court, so long

THE AWAKENING OF JAPAN

isolated from participation in affairs of state, the question of our national politics was doubly unintelligible, while their conservatism recoiled from the very mention of such outlandish notions. It was a difficult task for Hotta, who sincerely believed in the necessity of foreign intercourse and trade, to explain these things to a court which heard of them for the first time, and consequently his mission ended in failure. They asked many perplexing questions and could not understand why the citizens of a foreign nation should not obey the laws of the country in which they came to live.

The unpopularity of Hotta afforded an opportunity for the boudoir to obtain control of the government, and during his sojourn in Kioto the ladies of Yedo Castle replaced him by a pre-

CABINET AND BOUDOIR

mier who had agreed to side with them in the choice-of a future shogun. The new minister, lyi-Kamon, lord of Hi-kone, was the last exponent of Toku-gawa autocracy: he it was who accomplished the terrible coup d'etat of 1859. Though a choice of the boudoir, and representative of its policy, Hikone was possessed of no servile spirit. He was a loyal daimio of the old type, ready to carry out the wishes of his liege through fire or water. Descended from the greatest general among the forces of lyeyasu, his traditional loyalty rebelled at the encroachments of the Kioto court and the daimios upon the time-honored prestige of the Toku-gawas. To him the question of succession to the shogunate was purely a family matter for the Tokugawas to settle, and one in which no one else had

THE AWAKENING OF JAPAN

any right to interfere. To him, the signing of treaties with foreign nations was well within the prerogative intrusted to the Shogun from ancient days, and it was a mistake to have ever consulted the court nobles or the dai-mios about it. He recognized the fact that the country was undergoing a crisis, but believed that with firmness the authority of the Tokugawas could again be made thoroughly autocratic. It was with this determination that, in the summer of 1858, he answered the summons of the dying Shogun, who had been urged to send for him by the ladies of Yedo Castle.

The first act of Hikone after accepting the premiership was to declare the young prince lyemochi, of the house of Kishiu, who had been the choice of the dying Shogun, ruler instead of Keiki

CABINET AND BOUDOIR

of Mito, the candidate of the daimios. lyemochi, who was but thirteen at the time of his appointment, ruled as the thirteenth Shogun of the Tokugawas until the year 1866, when he died and was succeeded by Keiki. Hikone's second act was pubjicly to disgrace those dannios who had been recognized leaders of the opposition in regard to the question of succession. The old prince of Mito and the lord of Echizen were forced to resign their offices, and members of the Abe party, from Hotta downward, were degraded in rank. His third act was to sign commercial treaties with various Western nations, in utter disregard of the wishes of the Mikado, to whom a report of his actions was sent by the common post.

All these measures, and especially the last, were in the nature of bravado against national sentiment. The court highly resented the audacity of the new Tokugawa minister, and Kioto became the center where emissaries of the disaffected daimios met to conspire and plan countermoves. The prince of Mito received imperial instructions to call an assemblage of the daimios to reform the Tokugawa cabinet. Hi-kone, who watched all these proceedings through his spies, was not slow to move. In the spring of 1859 nearly forty of the more prominent agitators were arrested and either beheaded or imprisoned for high treason. All were famous men of the time, and among their number were included scholars, poets, and artists. One court lady, also im-pHcated, was exiled. Many of the kuges were compelled to shave their heads and retire from the world. The most deplorable result of this coup d'etat was the loss to Japan of a great number of men of remarkable genius. Among those beheaded were Yoshida-Shoyin of Choshiu, precursor and in-spirer of Kido and Marquis Ito, and Hashimoto-Sanai of Echizen, a statesman of a Mazzini-like intellect, for whose death alone the Tokugawa government was said to have deserved its downfall. Our Garibaldi, the great Saigo of Satsuma, had a hairbreadth escape from the hands of Hikone's minions.

This sudden display of despotism quelled the national spirit for a time, but the silence whicli followed was ominous. Assassination always lurks in the shadow of an absolute tyranny. In the late spring of 1860 it was snowing heavily and the light flakes mingled with the falhng cherry-blossoms. The road from the palace of the lord of Hikone to the Sakurada gate of Yedo Castle was completely deserted as lyi-Kamon and his unsuspecting retinue passed on their way to pay the usual morning homage to the Shogun. Suddenly they were attacked by seventeen ronins, mostly of the Mito clan, and Hikone was killed almost before his body-guard had time to draw their swords. The assassins fell upon their own weapons, leaving a few of their comrades to explain to the nearest authorities that their deed had been a stroke for national liberty and not an act of private vengeance.

Deplorable as this tragedy was, it had a helpful eiFect on the country, and showed that reawakened Japan was determined to resist to the utmost any attempts at the reenforcement of despotism. Perhaps a justification of such acts lies in the fact that assassination is the only weapon of a disarmed patriotism. No constitutional protest would have availed against the iron sway of Tokugawa autocracy. The icy structure of Tokugawa tyranny melted away like the snows of Sakurada beneath the warm blood of the devoted ronins.

A profound feeling of uneasiness possessed the nation, and the popular imagination was excited in various waj^s by those who had at heart the complete restoration of authority to the Mikado. Placards denouncing the usurpation of the Shogun were posted in public places by invisible hands. Mystic tablets foretelling the doom of the Tokugawas were reported to have been wafted from the heavens to various parts of the empire. Masked bands waylaid the official mail and intercepted the transport of government revenue, the money being given to the poor. A great number of samurai forsook their liege lord and assembled in Kioto to offer their swords for the service of the Mikado. The acts of these ronins were characterized more by symbolic demonstration than by open violence against the shogunate. To cite one instance of their methods: a band of ronins entered the mausoleum of the Ashikagas and decapitated the statues of the thirteen shoguns of that dynasty and displayed their heads near the Shi jo bridge. This childish act had a strange influence over the Japanese mind, with its Oriental love of sjTnbolism, and was even more potent than the Sakurada aiFair in arousing the feelings of the people. It spared us the horror of an assassination, yet had all the ghastly eloquence of one.

After the death of Hikone the Toku-gawa cabinet no longer possessed a minister able to cope with the situation, and its attempts at popular conciliation were interpreted as confessions of weakness. Ando-Tsushimanokami, who succeeded Hikone as senior member of the cabinet, prevailed upon the Kioto court to bestow the hand of the Princess Kazunomiya, sister of the Mikado, on the Shogun. This political marriage was celebrated in 1861 with great j^omp, but did not lessen the existing tension. Public sentiment against the Tokugawas had reached such a point that fictitious stories about the maltreatment of the royal bride were readily believed. The prime minister was even accused of holding the princess as a hostage for the acquiescence of the court in the despotic measures of his predecessor. The following year he was attacked by ronins while on his way to the palace of the Shogun, but the would-be assassins were unsuccessful in their attempt on his life. Ando, who was a fine swordsman, cut down two of his assailants while his body-guard despatched the rest. These repeated attacks on the Tokugawa ministers were significant of the tendency of events, and forty of the more powerful dai-mios received an imperial summons to protect Kioto. The throne once more became the real seat of authority, and Yedo Castle but the home of its chief vassal. The boudoir, in attempting to crush the cabinet, had dealt a deathblow to the entire Tokugawa government.

THE TRANSITION

THE eight years that intervene between the death of Hikone in 1860 and the Restoration of 1868, when his Majesty the present Emperor of Japan assumed the reins of government, are memorable for the wealtli of energy which was displayed by the nation in adopting a rapid series of political changes. The dragon-spirit ofi^ change was constantly urging the nation after new ideals. Even the busy years that followed the Restoration could not equal in activity this short period, into which were compressed the germs of all later movements. We are reminded of those great transition periods of European history when forms become formless in order to create new forms. Like the initiators of the Itahan Renaissance, we had to solve the double problem of restoring the old while absorbing the new. Like the much-abused French Revolution, so rich in idealization, our Restoration is characterized by an exuberant desire for self-sacrifice on the part of its enthusiasts. It was due to this feeling of patriotic ardor that the samurai voluntarily gave up his swords, the daimio his fiefs, and the Shogun his hereditary authority.

The turmoil of the Restoration was not confined to Kioto and Yedo, but found expression in all j)arts of the empire. Everywhere families were divided by their varying allegiance to the Mikado or to the Shogun, the son opposing the father, the younger brother the elder. Kioto became the headquarters of intrigue and the breeding-place of extreme views. The Restoration had really begun when the daimios were summoned to protect the imperial person, and now the court, strengthened by their presence at Kioto, began to dictate terms to the Shogun. There was no question of restitution of supreme authority to the Mikado, for this was a consummation universally desired and already half accomplished; but as regards the method of administering the government there were many opinions. Two great parties, the Federalists and the Imperialists, each representative of a different political system, gathered about the throne. These alternately gained the upper hand until both became united in a third party, the Unionists, which laid the foundations of our present administrative system.

The ascendancy of these different parties each in its turn marks the successive steps by which the political life of the nation was returning to its ancient form. We had now reached a point where the possibility of assuming an international position opened before us a mighty vista. The dragon was curving backward for his final spring. It was a curious example of social embryology that Japan should have assumed atavistic forms before its rebirth.

Of the two original j)arties, the Federalists, under the leadership of the lord of Satsuma, represented the various daimios. Their position prevented them from welcoming any abrupt change in the government, and they hoped for some sort of federation whereby they might control the sho-gunate. Their ideal government was that of the end of the sixteenth century, when, before the consolidation of the Tokugawa shogunate, the newly unified empire was governed by a council made up of five of the most powerful dairnios; in fact, they wished for a revival of the feudal age. Their foreign policy made a virtue of necessity, and, like the shogunate, accepted the inevitable in commercial relationships with the West.

The Imperialists sought their ideal further back in our history than the Federalists, and desired the restitution of imperial bureaucracy as it had existed before the feudal period. It was not only radical, but revolutionary in its propositions, inasmuch as it aimed at the abolition of the shogunate and even of the daimiates. Those who composed the Federal party were the kuges, hereditarily connected with the throne, the ronins, and the Shintoists, the ardor of the last augmented by religious zeal for the descendant of the Sun Goddess. The lord of Choshiu, whose family had long secretl\'7d'- nursed a feud with the Tokugawas, also joined the rank of the Federalists. All of these were fii'ed with a burning enthusiasm for the cause of the Mikado. They had no foreign policy except that of antagonism. This was due not so much to their hatred of the West as to their exasperation with the shogunate for signing treaties with the foreigner regardless of the wishes of the Mikado.

The Unionists, who later appeared on the scene, were men of advanced thought who considered that the unity of Japan should be accomplshed at any cost, and that the crisis through which we were passing involved international as well as national problems. All had received scholastic training, for the most part in the Oyomei School; they had also acquired a certain amount of Western knowledge, the assimilation of which the liberal policy of Abe-Isenokami had rendered possible. They were to be found even among the Tokugawa samurai, the late Count Katsu-Awa being a noteworthy example. The main strength of this party, however, lay in the young samurai of Satsuma, Choshiu, and Tosa, whose patriotism furnished the backbone of New Japan, and the survivors of whom now command deep respect as the " Elder Statesmen."

The Unionists, second to none in their adoration of the Mikado, worked for the full restoration of his sovereignty; but their theory of administration, in returning to the democratic ideas of ancient China, stretched still further back into antiquity even than those of the others. In the idealized > Confucian state all men were equal and the head of the government ruled, not on account of his descent, but by virtue of his personal rectitude. Wisdom was sought in a council of elders, and popular opinion was consulted in various ways. All should take up arms against an invasion; but as soon as war ceased the sword should be beaten again into the plowshare and the works of peace resumed. European and American republics, as at first understood by our scholars, reminded them curiously of 14<8

the Golden Age of the Celestial Land. In one of the letters of Sakuma-Sho-zan, a noted Unionist leader, he says, "It is wonderful that among the barbarians should be preserved the laws of the ancient sages!" Untutored as yet in the darker side of Western politics, they fell into ecstasies over those achievements of modern nations which seemed to them an actualization of their ideals. In George Washington they saw the Emperor Yaou of China relinquishing his throne to the ablest citizen of the realm. Wonder is the mother of knowledge. Treatises on international law were read with the same respect which was rendered to the codes of the Chow dynasty. JNIontes-quieu, with his triune theory of government, was hailed as the Book of Mencius. Far from despising the 14.9

<^:

West, the Unionists laid themselves at its feet. It was not the novelty but the similarity of what they found that attracted them. Sakuma-Shozan first proposed to the authorities the employment of European instructors in all branches of study. He was also the first Japanese who adopted European costume.

We may mention, in passing, that this idiosyncrasy of dress was actuated by a love of symbolism. It was the expression of a desire on the part of the progressionist to cast off the shackles of the decadent East and identify himself with the advance of Western civilization. Our kimono meant leisure, while the European dress meant activity, and it became the uniform of the army of progress, like the chapeau rouge in revolutionary France. Xow-150

adays a reaction has set in, and native costume is more generally worn by the progressives. Few of our ladies affect European costume except at court.

Sakuma-Shozan paid dearly for his pro-foreign leanings: in 1866 he was assassinated at Kioto by the ronins of the imperial party. Yet despite conservative antagonism, Western knowledge became more and more sought after as time advanced, until it has now become an inherent part of our national culture. It must always be re-^ membered, however, that the original movement toward the acquirement of foreign knowledge was fostered by the historic spirit. If there had been no common point of contact, an Oriental race like ours would never have adopted Occidental ideas with the enthusiasm that we did.

THE AWAKENING OF JAPAN

Of the three parties above mentioned, the Federals were at first in the ascendant. In 1862 two imperial embassies, escorted by the lords of Satsuma and Tosa, left Kioto for Yedo, carrying orders to the Shogmi to give the higher positions under his administration to certain powerful daimios, and furthermore commanding him to pay personal homage to the throne, a ceremony neglected since the days of the fourth Shogun. The Tokugawas had now no power to refuse, and as the result of these commands Prince Keiki was made chief adviser of the Shogun, the lord of Nabeshima his tutor, the lord of Echizen prime minister of the cabinet, and the lord of Awa director of military affairs. The first action of the new cabinet was to abolish the custom by which the daimios

THE TRANSITION

were obliged to leave hostages at Yedo and they themselves periodically to pay homage to the Shogun, both of which usages formed so important a part of the Tokugawa system. Another of their reforms was the replacement of the Tokugawa garrison at Kioto by one under the command of a Federal daimio. Their choice for this position fell on the lord of Aidzu, who later stood forth as the champion of the Federal policy after most of the other daimios had joined the Unionists.

Beyond carrying through these reforms, the Federal party accomplished but little. The program of instituting radical changes while preserving the Tokugawa rule soon placed them in a dilemma, while petty jealousies and dissensions began to spring up in their

THE AWAKENING OF JAPAN

ranks. The lord of Satsuma, who alone might have controlled the dai-mios, had to return to his territory on account of complications with the English. By the spring of 1863 we find the Federals thoroughly disunited, all of the daimios who had taken office the previous year having resigned except Prince Keiki and the lord of Aidzu.

Meanwhile the Imperialists were becoming anxious over the turn of events. To them the daimios seemed to be lacking in loyalty to the Mikado. They even suspected Satsuma of trying to supplant the Tokugawas. The Federal attitude of complacency toward the foreigners was repugnant to them as showing a disregard of the imperial wishes. The disintegration of the Federal party now offered an opportunity

THE TRANSITION

for the Imperialists to take the helm of state. In April, 1863, they obtained imperial authority to close the ports and expel the foreigners, a measure which the Tokugawas refused to sanction and which the daimios would not take seriously. The Imperialists, however, were not daunted by this rebuff, and the lord of Choshiu showed his contempt of Tokugawa authority by firing at the foreign vessels which passed the shores of his territory in their passage through the Strait of Bakan.

This rash act raised the opposition of the Federal party and caused its re-consolidation. Seven of the younger kuges were accused of surreptitiously obtaining the imperial sanction to this anti-foreign demonstration and were obliged to flee for their lives, while the samurai and ronins of the Choshiu clan were forbidden the city of Kioto. They attempted to take the Federal guards of the palace gates by surprise in order to make appeal directly to the Mikado, but were repulsed with great loss. Attempted uprisings in three diifferent parts of the country met with failure, and the whole body of Imperialists had to seek refuge in Choshiu. A joint army led by the lords of Owari and Echizen soon surrounded the fugitives and compelled the lord of Choshiu to execute three of his chief officers as an atonement for his misdemeanor, while he was obliged to retire into a monastery co await further orders. Owari and Echizen were not desirous of inflicting further punishment, and the invading armies were soon withdrawn. The lord of Aidzu was dissatisfied with this comparatively

light form of chastisement, and prevailed upon the Shogun to lead in person a second invasion of Choshiu.

It was now that the Unionist party was formed. In their opinion, it was suicidal for the nation to be involved in internal disputes when foreign interference might be expected at any time. A second invasion of Choshiu, if successful, would reinstate the Tokuga-was in power, something which neither the Federals nor the Imperialists were desirous of bringing about. The initiative came from the lord of Tosa, who succeeded in reconciling the leaders of the rival clans of Satsuma and Choshiu. A triple alliance was secretly formed by these three daimios.

The Tokugawa army started from Yedo for the second invasion of Choshiu without the support of the Fed-

eral daimios, most of whom, with the exception of Aidzu, had ah'eady fallen under the influence of the Unionists and lent only their nominal assistance to the expedition. The golden fan of lyeyasu, hereditary insignia of the To-kugawas, which had carried all before it in the bloody battles of the sixteenth century, was at last to meet with defeat. Outgeneraled at every point, the To-kugawa army was unable to stand against the determined soldiers of Choshiu and had to beat an ignominious retreat. To add to the troubles of the Tokugawas, the Shogun died in the winter of 1866, shortly before the passing away of Komei Tenno, the imperial father of our reigning Majesty. This event gave an excuse to the Tokugawas for concluding a truce, which, however, virtually yielded the victory to the

lord of Choshiu. The seven court nobles who had sought refuge in Choshiu were allowed to return and were reinstated in their former rank. It was about this time that Marquis ^ Ito and other students who had been in Western countries returned from abroad and were welcomed by the Unionist leaders on account of the knowledge they had thus acquired. The party was now well equipped with ideas of constructive progress and constitutional government.

Prince Keiki, formerly a candidate for the shogunate and later adviser of the Shogun, was himself called upon to become the last of the shoguns, but the time had long passed when he might have had an opportunity of proving his ability. True to the principles inculcated by his father, the prince of ^Nlito,

his supreme devotion was to the Mikado, and he was convinced of the futility of trying longer to maintain the struggling fortunes of his own house. It needed no persuasion to induce him to give up his title and to restore entire authority to the throne. He was, in fact, unconsciously a thorough Unionist at heart. His most trusted counselor, the late Count Katsu-

Awa, was one of the Unionist leaders, though the rest of his vassals and daimios were, like the lord of Aidzu, Federals of the most pronounced type. It is said that when, in the fall of 1867, the envoys of the lord of Tosa came to urge his resignation, he bade them wait and at once drew up the memorable document in which he relinquished all the powers which had been intrusted to his family for nearly three hundred years. 160

THE TRANSITION

The lord of Aidzu and some of the Tokugawa samurai objected to this sudden surrender of the shogunate and raised revolts in Osaka and the northern provinces. . But, bereft of their leader, the Shogun, they were unable to make eiFective resistance to the Unionist army under the joint command of the great Saigo of Sat-suma and Omura of Choshiu. In the following year, after some desperate battles, they were all reduced to submission. Japan once more bowed to the military authority of the Mikado. The Restoration was complete.

RESTORATION AND REFORMATION

THE Restoration was at the same time a reformation. In emerging from an Asiatic hermitage to take our stand upon the broad stage of the world, we were obliged to assimilate much that the Occident offered for our advancement and at the same time to resuscitate the classic ideals of the East. The idea of the reformation is clearly expressed in the imperial declaration of 1868 in which his present jMajesty, after ascending the throne, stated that national obligations should be regarded from the broad standpoint of universal humanity. As the word signifies, our restoration 162

RESTORATION —REFORMATION

was essentially a return. The govern-^ ment once again assumed the form of an imperial bureaucracy, such as had existed before the rise of feudalism over seven hundred years ago. The first act of the new government was to reestablish all the ancient offices, together with their former nomenclature, while many long forgotten functions and ceremonies were revived and Shintoism was proclaimed as the religion of the imperial household. Posthumous honors were conferred on loyalists who, like Masa-shige, had served the cause of the court during the former shogunates, and the descendants of many of them were ennobled.

Yet these revivals of past conditions
were tempered with the new spirit of
freedom and equality. The JNIikado,
while pronouncing Shintoism to be the

THE AWAKENING OF JAPAN

religion of the household, granted liberty of conscience to the entire nation, and Christianity was freed from the interdiction under which it had lain since the Jesuit insurrection of the seventeenth century. The class distinction between nobles, samurai, and commoners was nominally retained, and the dai-mios and kuges were given titular rank according to the fine grades of the old Chinese system. A new aristocracy even was created. All class privileges, however, were abolished, and all, from the princes and the marquises down to the abhorred yettas (who to-day bear the nickname of the "New Commoners "), were made equal in the eye of the law, while examinations for the civil service were thrown open to every one. The object of those who conducted the reformation was so to fuse together the 164

RESTORATION—REFORMATION

hardened strata of Tokugawa social life that the entire nation might participate in the glory and responsibilities of the Restoration. There were four mail lines along which the work of preparing the nation to meet the problem of modern hfe was carried. These were, first, constitutional government; second, liberal education; third, universal military service; and fourth, the elevation of womanhood.

Constitutional government has been deemed impracticable for Eastern nations, and in Turkey it was a sad failure. With us, however, since the assembling of our first parliament the principles and ordinances of the state have been so well carried out that we can safely affirm the experimental age to have been passed and constitutional government to have become an inherent part of our political consciousness. We may have had occasional stormy debates and divisions, a phase of affairs not unknown in the conduct of Western national assemblies; but whenever threatened with foreign complications, all factions have invariably united in support of the cabinet. The successful working of the new system is partly due, no doubt, to an inherent power of self-government exemplified in the administration of many of our previous institutions, and partly to the fact that the nation had long been preparing for the responsibility of self-government.

In 1867, as soon as the Shogun had resigned his office, the Unionist ministry created two councils, one composed of the leading daimios and kuges, the other of representative samurai from various daimiates. When his Majesty

RESTORATION—REFORMATION

the present Emperor ascended the throne in 1868 and proclaimed the Restoration, he declared the establishment of a national assembly in which important affairs of state should be decided by public opinion. In 1875 a senate was created, to which all contemplated legislation had to be submitted by the cabinet, and this was soon followed by the establishment of the Court of Final Appeal. Thus were inaugurated the three principal factors in the conduct of a constitutional government, namely, the executive, legislative, and judicial bodies. In 1879 the senate passed a law creating in each local prefecture an assembly in which representatives elected by the taxpayers were to decide the annual expenditures and taxation of the province. In 1881 an imperial proclamation announced that the Constitution

THE AWAKENING OF JAPAN

would go into effect in 1890, and accordingly in February of that year it was duly promulgated. Our diet consists of the House of Commons and a House of Peers, the latter an outgrowth of the senate established in 1875. It is significant that our Constitution was the voluntary gift of the Mikado, and not, as in the case of some European nations, one forced from the sovereign by the people. Consistent with Eastern traditions, our democracy is an accretion, not an eruption.

The question of education for the people held a prominent place in the imperial declaration of 1868, the Mikado commanding the acquisition of knowledge from all sources throughout the world. We have already mentioned the existence in Tokugawa days of elementary schools for the commoners and

RESTORATION—REFORMATION

academies of learning for the higher classes. These were now systematically organized so that they might furnish the nation with the knowledge necessary for carrying out the obligations of its new environment. Elementary education was made compulsory for all boys and girls above six years of age, and normal schools were established in each of the provinces to supply them with teachers. In our educational system of to-day, next above the elementary schools come the middle schools, in which a liberal education is given and pupils are prepared for entering the higher institutions of learning. There are also special schools for those desirous of entering the navy or army, agriculture, industrial science, commerce, or the arts and crafts, while the imperial university includes colleges of law, literature, medicine, engineer-

THE AWAKENING OF JAPAN

ing, and science. Female education is not neglected, though, in accordance with Eastern custom, it is given separately. A few years ago a ladies' university was started in Tokio. The study of one of the European languages is compulsory in all except the elementary schools—that of English being the one generally required. A great number of Americans and Europeans are employed to give instruction, and thousands of young men and women study abroad either at their own or the government's expense. Our eagerness to acquire Western learning has prompted hosts of our young men to seek menial work in foreign countries,—service, according to Confucian notions, not being considered derogatory. The ethical training given to the rising generation is based on the teachings of earlier days.

RESTORATION—REFORMATION

The imperial manifesto which formulated the national code of morality, after summing up the universal principles of ethics, concludes with these words: " These are the teachings of our imperial ancestors, and this is the path followed by your ancestors." It is hardly necessary to add that the fruits of our newly acquired knowledge are all consecrated in intense devotion to the Mikado.

Our system of military service has proved more potent than any other factor in strengthening national loyalism. It has, in fact, transformed the commoner into a samurai. Conscription had obtained in Japan long before the rise of feudalism, and its practice was merely revived in 1870 on German and French lines. According to the present system, every male at twenty years of age is liable to be drafted for three years' service with the colors, and after that for a service of five years each in the first and second reserves. In case of extreme emergency the whole nation may be called to arms. The officers, trained in special schools and staff colleges, come mostly from samurai families, and their traditional code of life has permeated the entire new army. For the nation at large the social distinction of many centuries has thrown a halo about the sworded class, while current fiction and drama have for the last fifty years so idealized the patriotic soldier that the peasant conscript on entering the ranks feels himself ennobled not only in his own estimation but in that of his brethren; he is now a man of the sword, the soul of honor. He is fairly intelligent, thanks to the village school, soon mastering his tactics and imbibing that profound sense of duty which is the essence of samuraihood. At first, on account of his heretofore peaceful life, there were some misgivings about his courage; but the baptism of fire proved him able to take his place beside the best of the samurai. The contempt of death displayed by our conscripts is not founded, as some Western writers suppose, on the hope of a future reward. We preach no Valhalla or Moslem heaven awaiting our departed heroes; for the teachings of Buddhism promise in the next life but a miserable incarnation to the slayer of man. It is a sense of duty alone that causes our men to march to certain death at the word of command. Behind all lies devotion to the sovereign and love of country. Our conscript but follows the historic example of tliose heroes who ever gave themselves as willing sacrifices for the good of the nation. If he sometimes offers his blood too freely, it is through an exuberance of patriotic love; for love, like death, recognizes no limits.

Another important feature of the reformation lay in the exaltation of womanhood. The Western attitude of profound respect toward the gentler sex exhibits a beautiful phase of refinement which we are anxious to emulate. It is one of the noblest messages that Christianity has given us. Christianity originated in the East, and, except as regards womanhood, its modes of thought are not new to Eastern minds. As the new religion spread westward through Europe, it naturally became influenced by the idiosyncrasies of the various converted nations, so that the poetry of the German forest, the adoration of the Virgin in the middle centuries, the age of chivalry, the songs of the troubadours, the delicacy of the Latin nature, and, above all, the clean manhood of the Anglo-Saxon race, probably all contributed their share toward the idealization of woman.

In Japan, woman has always commanded a respect and freedom not to be found elsewhere in the East. We have never had a Salic law, and it is from a female divinity, the Sun-goddess, that our Mikado traces his lineage. During many of the most brilliant epochs in our ancient history we were under the laile of a female sovereign. Our Empress Zingo personally led a victorious army into Korea, and it was Empress Suiko who inaugurated the refined culture of the Nara period. Female sovereigns ascended the throne in their own right even when there were male candidates, for we considered woman in all respects as the equal of man. In our classic literature we find the names of more great authoresses than authors, while in feudal days some of our amazons charged with the bravest of the Kamakura knights. /QAs time advanced and Confucian theories became more potent in molding our social customs, woman was relegated from public life and confined to what was considered by the Chinese sage as her proper sphere, the household. Our inherent respect for the rights of womanhood, however, remained the same, and as late as the year 1630 a female mikado, Meisho-Tenno, ascended the throne of her fathers. Until after the Restoration, a knowledge of such martial exercises as fencing and jiujitsuwas considered part of the education of a samurai's daughter, and is, indeed, still so considered among many old families. Among the commoners the various industries and trades have always been open to women as they are to-day, while we have already seen how, in spite of her apparent seclusion, the Tokugawa lady impressed her individuality on the state. Buddhism has its worship for the eternal feminine and Confucianism has always inculcated a reverence for womanhood, teaching that the wife should always be treated with the respect due to a guest or friend.

We have never hitherto, however, learned to offer any special privileges to woman. Love has never occupied an important place in Chinese literature; and in the tales of Japanese chivalry, the samurai, although ever at the service of the weak and oppressed, gave his help quite irrespective of sex. To-day we are convinced that the elevation of woman is the elevation of the race. She is the epitome of the past and the reservoir of the future, so that the responsibilities of the new social life which is dawning on the ancient realms of the Sun-goddess may be safely intrusted to her care. Since the Restoration we have not only confirmed the equality of sex in law, but have adopted that attitude of respect which the West pays to woman. She now possesses all the rights of her Western sister, though she does not care to insist upon them; for almost all of our women still consider the home, and not society, as their proper sphere.

Time alone can decide the future of the Japanese lady, for the question of womanhood is one involving the whole social life and its web of convention. In the East woman has always been worshiped as the mother, and all those honors which the Christian knight brought in homage to his lady-love, the samurai laid at his mother's feet. It is not that the wife is less adored, but that maternity is holier. Again, our woman love to serve her husband; for service is the noblest expression of affection, and love rejoices more in giving than in receiving. In the harmony of Eastern society the man consecrates himself to the state, the child to the parent, and the wife to the husband.

After the successful accomplishment of the Restoration, there still remained for nearly thirty years one bitter drop in our cup of happiness. That was the question of treaty revision. We had established a constitutional government and a complete educational system; we had reorganized our army and navy and joined the Geneva Convention; we had remodeled our civil law code and developed extensive conmiercial relations with the rest of the world, yet the foreign powers persistently refused to revise the obsolete treaties signed under the Tokugawa shogunate. We did not complain of the low rate of our customs-duties, though with our growing commerce this meant a heavy loss to us, but of the jurisdiction exercised by exterritorial courts. Japan was restored, but not entirely freed. There were spots in the JNIikado's realm which his sovereignty could not reach. The Westerner, who has never known the presence of a foreign consular court in his own country, cannot be expected to

RESTORATIO^N—REFORMATION

realize the anguish that they cause to those upon whom they are imposed. It is not that the decisions of these courts are unfair, but misunderstandings are always arising through the existence of race distinctions, while the fact that foreign laws should be administered at all is in itself a condemnation of the law and justice of the country, and is necessarily a humiliation to any self-respecting nation. Since the beginning of the Restoration the efforts of our government have been constantly directed toward the abolishment of this system, but every proposal of ours was either met by the foreign powers with a peremptory refusal or elicited some exorbitant demand in exchange. The United States of America, it is true, agreed to a revision if all the other powers would join, but this was something

THE AWAKENING OF JAPAN

which Europe was sure not to do. It was a hard task for us to convince the West that an Eastern nation could successfully assume the responsibilities of an enlightened people. It was not until our war with China in 1894-95 had revealed our military strength as well as our capacity to maintain a high standard of international morality, that Europe consented to put an end to her exterritorial jurisdiction in Japan. It is one of the painful lessons of history that civilization, in its progress, often climbs over the bodies of the slain.

Great are the struggles that we have had to undergo during these last few decades. In the turmoil of the reformation the swing of the pendulum was often extreme, causing the passage of many unnecessary if not actually harmful measures. We have often stood be-

RESTORATION—REFORMATION

wildered in the mid-stream of conflicting opinions, watching with dismay the shifting sand-banks of the half-reahzed constantly changing with the currents of subconscious thought. All the ridiculousness of paradox, all the cruelty of dilemma, were ours. We might have laughed had we not wept. Conservative reactions caused riots and local rebellions in which we lost many of the greatest pioneers of our reformation, and radical zealots often cut short with their swords the career of some far-sighted leader. We must be ever thankful that the helm was held throughout by hands strong enough to keep the ship of state steadily on its course, in spite of storms and contrary currents.

THE REINCARNATION

PESSIMISTS declare that the Old Japan is no more. They hold that in her modernization she has lost her individuality and broken the thread of her historic unity. Eminent European writers have regarded the present condition of aiFairs in Japan as transient and impermanent, a strange freak of orientalism sooner or later doomed to disintegration. They image our mutability in the straw sandals which we change at every stage of a journey; our disregard of all permanence in the wooden houses that are daily swept away by conflsigrations. To them everything

THE REINCARNATION

Japanese lacks solidity and stability, from the constantly vibrating land in which we dwell to the philosophy of Buddhism teaching the evanescence of all things.

It is true that the imperative needs of our sudden transformation from the old to the new life have swept away many landmarks of Old Japan; yet in spite o changes, we have still been able to remain true to our former ideals; though our sandals be changed, our journey continues; though our houses be burnt, our cities remain; and the earthquake but shows the virility of the mighty fish that upholds our island empire/

It should be remembered that in Eastern philosophy the poetrj'^ of things is more real and vital than mere facts

1 Japanese folk-lore teaches that earthquakes are caused by the movements of a huge fish which bears the islands of Japan upon its back.

THE AWAKENING OF JAPAN

and events. Buddhism, which taught the transitory nature of the mundane, never for a moment ceased to teach the immutabihty of the soul. Since the earhest dawn of history our national patriotism and devotion to the Mikado show a consistent tenacity of ancient ideals, while the fact that we have ^^^reserved the arts and customs of an-K/cient China and India long after they have become lost in the lands of their birth is sufficient testimony to our reverence for traditions. Our conservatism is well typified by the Shinto temple of Ise, where the Sun-goddess, founder of our imperial line, is forever worshiped. That holiest shrine of our ancestrism remains to-day as perfect in its pristine beauty as it was twenty centuries ago, being rebuilt every twenty years on an alternate site in its exact original form. 186

THE REINCARNATION

The world may, perhaps, laugh at our love of monotony, but can never accuse us of a lack of constancy. Our individuality has been preserved from submersion beneath the mighty tide of Western ideas by the same national characteristics which ever enabled us to remain true to ourselves in spite of repeated influxes of foreign thought. From time immemorial the civilizations of China and India have silted over Korea and the adjacent coasts of Japan. The Tang dynasty flooded us with its pantheism and harmonism, while under the Sung dynasty new elements of romanticism and individualism were carried to our shores. From the dualistic theories of the Hinayana ^ to the ultra-monistic doctrines of Bodhidharma,' In-

^ Southern school of Buddhism, or Lesser Vehicle. ^ An Indian monk who came to China in the sixth century and started the early form of Zen.

THE AWAKENING OF JAPAN

dia has dowered us with a wealth of religion and philosophy. Different and conflicting as were these various schools of thought, Japan has welcomed them all and assimilated whatever ministered to her mental needs, incorporating the xgift as an integral part of her thought-inheritance. The hearth of our ancient ideals was ever guarded by a careful eclecticism, while the broad fields of our national life, enriched by the fertile deposits of each successive inundation, burst forth into fresher verdure. The expenditure of thought involved in synthesizing the different elements of Asiatic culture has given to Japanese philosophy and art a freedom and virility unknown to India and China. It is thus due to past training that we are able to comprehend and appreciate more easily than our neighbors 188

THE REINCARNATION

those elements of Western civilization which it is desirable that we should acquire. Accustomed to accept the new without sacrificing the old, our adoption of Western methods has not so greatly affected the national life as is generally supposed. The same eclecticism which had chosen Buddha as the spiritual and Confucius as the moral guide, hailed modern science as the beacon of material progress. Our efforts to master certain phases of Western development have resulted in an increase of industrial activity and the introduction of scientific sanitation and surgery, while our methods of communication and transportation have been greatly improved and the ordinarj^ comforts of life are much more universally enjoyed than ever before. Development along such lines, however, has but little effect on our national character beyond acting as a stimulus for further efforts.

Again, the adoption of Western political and social customs has not necessitated so great a change on our part as might at first seem apparent. Our past . experience taught us to choose in West-'ern institutions only what was consistent with our Eastern nature. It must be remembered that in spite of the seeming demarcation of the East and the West, all human development is fundamentally the same, and that in the vast range of Asiatic history there can be found almost every variety of social usage. We have already alluded to that ancient Confucian state which suggested democracy to the Unionists. The five grades of nobility from duke to baron were known in the Chow dynasty three thousand years ago. Slavery was abolished by the Hang dynasty during the first century of the Christian era. So-ciahstie theories concerning the equal distribution of propert\'7d^ and government management of agricultural products, were carried into actual practice during the Hang and Sung dynasties. Modern German idealism was anticipated in India many ages ago, while Christianity has many parallelisms in Buddhism. The modern European tendency toward the demarcation of the church from the state, as well as the civil-service examination system, has existed in China since early days. It was on ac count of these and many other points of resemblance between Western and Asiatic civilizations that Japan was able to borrow much from Europe and America without violating her sense of tradition. One who looks beneath the surface of things can see, in spite of her modern garb, that the heart of Old Japan is still beating strongly. Our Civil Code, which embodies the spirit of Western law, incorporates to a great extent the customs and usages of our past. Our Constitution, though it may seem similar to many Western constitutions, is founded on our ancient system of government, and even finds its prototype in the days of the gods. The Japanese Renaissance, which began in the eighteenth century, has never stayed its course. Armed with more systematic methods, our scholars still pursue their research into ancient art and literature. The Historical Bureau of Tokio University has akeady collected an immense quantity of material for the reconstruction of our annals. The Imperial Archaeological Commission has, in the last fifteen years, ransacked the monasteries throughout the whole extent of the empire, and confuted many of the traditions of the Tokugawa critics. Rare Chinese books are eagerly sought after, an extremely valuable collection being recently acquired from the imperial archives of Peking. An interest in Sanskrit literature has also arisen, and the Max Miiller library has been recently purchased and brought to Tokio, while Buddhism and Confucianism are studied with even greater zest than they were at the outset of the Restoration. Old customs and ceremonies are being revived, and a knowledge of our ancient etiquette forms as much a part of a gentleman's training as ever it did, the tendencj^ of democracy being only to make it more universal than before. The tea-ceremony and flower-arrangement have again become common features in the life of our ladies. Classic music and drama are widely studied even by people of European education. It may not, perhaps, be generally known that the ancient ceremonial functions of the court are kept up to-day without any alteration in form. As a notable instance of this, we may call attention to the fact that the declaration of war with Russia was announced to the Sun-goddess by a distinguished envoy from the Mikado, and a special guard was detailed for service at the shrine in Ise during the continuance of hostilities. As Hakuraku discerned the real horse, so may he who perceives the real spirit of things see in current events the reincarnation of Old Japan. In the thoroughness and minutiae of our preparations for war, he will recognize the same hands whose untiring patience gave its exquisite finish to our lacquer. In the tender care bestowed upon our stricken adversary of the battle-field will be found the ancient courtesy of the samurai, who knew " the sadness of things" and looked to his enemy's wound before his own. The ardor that" leads our sailors into daring enterprises', is inspired by the Neo-Confucian doctrine which teaches that to know is to do. The calmness with which our people have met the exigencies of a national crisis is a heritage from those disciples of Buddha who in the silence of the monastery meditated on change.

All that is vital and representative in our contemporary art and literature is the revivified expression of the national school, not imitation of European models. The brilliant creations of our leading novelists, Koda-Rohan and the late Ozaki-Koyo, are based on a revival of the style of the seventeenth century. The name of the lamented Danjuro, one of the greatest actors that the world has ever seen, is inseparably connected with our historical drama. The well-known ceramists, Takemoto-Hayata, Makuzu-Kozan, and Seifu-Yohei, may be considered as wonderful as the old Chinese masters whose secrets they have discovered. Natsuo, Zesshin, Hogai, and Gaho illustriously prove that the spirit of our ancient art still lives. We do not mean to say that the study of European art and literature is in any way injurious or even undesirable, but that so far its results can in no way compare with the achievements of the native school.

It is a matter of no small wonder that our national art should have survived amid the adverse surroundings in which it found itself. The philistine nature of industrialism and the restlessness of material progress are inimical to Eastern art. The machinery of competition imposes the monotony of fashion instead of the variety of life. The cheap is worshiped in place of the beautiful, while the rush and struggle of modern existence give no opportunity for the leisure required for the crystallization of ideals. Patronage is no longer even the sign of individual bad taste. Music is criticized through the eye, a picture through the ear.

The possibility that Japanese art may become a thing of the past is a matter of sympathetic concern to the esthetic community of the West. It should be known that our art is suffering not merely from the purely utilitarian trend of modern life, but also from an inroad of Western ideas. The demand of the Western market for dubious art goods, together with the constant criticism of our standard of taste, has told upon our individuality. Our difficulty lies in the fact that Japanese art stands alone in the world, without immediate possibility of any accession or reinforcement from kindred ideals or technique. We no longer have the benefit of a living art in China to excite our rivalry and urge us on to fresh endeavors. On the other hand, the unfortunately contemptuous attitude which the average Westerner assumes toward everything connected with Oriental civilization tends to destroy our self-confidence in regard to our canons of art. Those European and American connoisseurs who appreciate our efforts may not realize that the

THE REINCARNATION

West, as a whole, is constantly preaching the sujjeriority of its own culture and art to those of the East. Japan stands alone against all the world. It is but natural that the weak-spirited among us follow the trend of world-opinion and desert the ranks of conservative upholders of our national school. The delight of some of our gilded youths in the latest cut of a London tailor or the last novelty from Paris is one of the pathetic indications of an attempted protective coloring against the universal condemnation of Eastern customs.

Japanese art has done wonders in remaining true to itself in spite of the odds it has had to face. We trust and hope that the tenacious vitality which it has evinced, in spite of the overwhelming occidentalism of the last four decades,

I

THE AWAKENING OF JAPAN

will keep Japanese art intact in the future. Every accession to our national self-confidence is a strong incentive to the preservation of national ideals. A great reaction toward native customs and art has been manifested since our victory over China ten years ago. We hope that our success over a stronger adversary than China will give us a still deeper self-confidence. We shall be ready more than ever to learn and assimilate what the West has to offer, but we must remember that our claim to respect lies in remaining faithful to our own ideals.

JAPAN AND PEACE

WE have been repeatedly accused of belligerent designs and expansive ambitions. Perhaps to European nations, with their traditions of conquest and colonization, it may be inconceivable that we are not animated by the same spirit of aggrandizement that has often led them into war. But to any one who cares to study the history of our foreign policy nothing can be clearer than the constancy of our desire for the maintenance of peace, our final recourse to war being forced upon us by the necessity of safeguarding our national existence. The very na-

THE AWAKENING OF JAPAN

ture of our civilization, in fact, prohibits aggression against foreign nations. Confucianism, which is an epitome of the agricultural civilization of China, is essentially self-contained and non-aggressive in its nature. The fertility of the vast plains wherein the teachings of Confucius were followed rendered any overstepping of their natural boundaries unnecessary. The message of the sage made love of the soil and consecration of labor go hand in hand. He and his followers taught the homely and the patriarchal virtues of mf kness and harmony. Later came Buddhism to reinforce the root-idea of contentment and self-restraint. Not once during the whole of their hoary history do we find the native dynasties of China and India ever coming into collision with each other. The only oc-

JAPAN AND PEACE

casion on which China ever menaced Japan was when in the twelfth century her own Mongol conquerors tried to impose their authority upon us.

Japan, though originally a maritime nation, had through the influence of Confucianism and Buddhism long ago become, like her neighbors, self-contained, seeking the fulfilment of her destinies within the narrow limits of her island empire. The fact that in the eighth century we had given up our ancient dominion over Korea, proves how deeply the continental idea had become a part of our national consciousness. The Korean peninsula had probably originally been colonized by us during prehistoric ages. Archseological remains in Korea are of exactly the same type as those found in our primitive dolmens. The Korean language remains, even to-day, the nearest allied to ours of all the Asiatic tongues. Our earliest traditions tell of the god Sosano, brother of our imperial ancestress, settling in Korea; and Dankun, first king of that country, is considered by some historians to have been his son. The third century discloses our Empress Zhingo leading an invasion of the peninsula in order to re-estabhsh our sovereignty, threatened by the rise of a number of small independent kingdoms. Our annals are filled until the eighth century with accounts of our protection over colonies. From this time onward, however, a great change comes over Japan, and all our energy is expended in rehgious fervor. This age, which witnessed the erection of innumerable monasteries and the casting of the colossal Buddha of Nara, saw the last of our Korean colonies allowed to perish, her appeals for help unheeded by the mother-country.

The attempted jNIongol invasion of the thirteenth century kindled in us a feeling of animosity toward the Koreans who led the Chinese vanguard. Our only act of retaliation, however, consisted in the unique expedition of the Taiko Hideyoshi, who, in the sixteenth century, led an army into Korea to measure swords with those whom he considered as his hereditar\'7d^ enemies. But national sentiment had long lost sympathy with any idea of foreign conquest, and the Taiko's army was presently recalled at his death. The only result of this extraordinary expedition was the sending, during subsequent Tokugawa days, of envoys from the Korean sovereign to pay the homage of a tributary king to each newly appointed shogun— a homage equally oiFered to the Chinese emperors. This ceremony continued till the days of the Restoration, but we never thought of availing ourselves of the right impMed by it to interfere in continental politics. On the contrary, we prided ourselves upon our complete isolation from the rest of the world, and did not even seek to renew those diplomatic amenities with China which had ceased after the Taiko's expedition.

The Tokugawa policy of non-interference in continental aif airs is well ex-emphfied in the refusal of aid to the celebrated Koxinga, a patriotic general of the Ming dynasty, who drove the Dutch out of Formosa and for three generations held it against the Manchu conquerors of China. The governors of all other provinces surrendered, and he alone upheld the remnant of Ming authority. Half a Japanese himself, being the son of a Ming refugee by a Nagasaki woman, he pleaded his birth as a reason for asking for an alUance and reinforcements from the Japanese. Several young daimios, together with quite a number of samurai, fired by his appeal, wished to volunteer, but the To-kugawa authorities absolutely refused to allow them to do so.

Our relations with China and Korea since the Restoration of 1868 are strikingly illustrative of our traditional policy of peace and non-aggression. When we emerged from our sleep of three centuries international conditions were changed indeed! Events were taking place in Asia which threatened our very existence. No Eastern nation could hope to maintain its independence unless it was able to defend itself from outside attack. Natural barriers were as naught before the advance of science. The Yellow Sea and the Korean straits, which we formerly considered as invincible obstacles to aggression from the continent, amounted to little since the introduction of fast war-ships and long-range ordnance. Any hostile power in occupation of the peninsula might easily throw an army into Japan, for Korea lies Hke a dagger ever pointed toward the very heart of Japan. Moreover, the independence of Korea and Manchuria is economically necessary to the preservation of our race, for starvation awaits our ever-increasing population if it be deprived of its legitimate outlet in the sparsely cultivated areas of these countries. To-day the Muscovites have laid their hands on these territories, with none but us to offer any resistance. Under

these circumstances, we are compelled to regard our ancient domain of Korea as lying within our lines of legitimate national defense. It was when the independence of the peninsula was threatened by China in 1894 that we were compelled to go to war with the latter country. It was for this same independence that we fought Russia in 1904.

There were several occasions when we might have taken possession of Korea, but we forbore, in the face of strong provocation, because our wishes were for peace. We must remember that the historic spirit that created the Restoration also recalled the fact that Korea was originally a Japanese province, and in the Tokugawa days paid tribute to the shogunate. A camis belli was not wanting in the early seventies of the last century, for Korea labored under

strange delusions, and not only refused to recognize the government of the Restoration, but heaped insults upon us. Much less cause of provocation than ours has often been taken as a ground for aggression by European nations. The divisions in the cabinet of 1873 and the rebellion caused by the secessionists of Satsuma in 1879 were the result of disputes between the war and peace parties, in which the latter always came out victorious. At that time the West had not the keen interest in the East that she has since acquired, and would not have interfered with our actions. The members of the war party urged that the unique moment had arrived when Japan might assume control of Korea and lay at rest forever the danger of her falling into the hands of some other power. To them Korea had al-

ways been a tributary nation, and we would be but confirming already existing rights. Perhaps if the Korean question had been then settled, all the bloodshed of the Chinese and Russian wars might have been avoided.

The Mikado's chief advisers, together with a majority of those who had a voice in the government, were strongly opposed to the views of the war party. In their eyes the Restoration had a higher significance than could be found in aggrandizement at the expense of neighboring countries. To them it represented the principles of justice and humanity, liberalism, and the elevation of the Japanese race. Its very key-notes should be nobleness and self-sacrifice, the virtues of the samurai enlarged into those of the nation. The lives of those statesmen who, like Okubo-Toshimichi,

Kido-Koyin, and Prince Iwakura, held to these lofty ideals gave its moral tone to the present Japanese government and are eloquent of unselfishness and purity. Their simplicity and determination are characteristic of those enlightened spirits who appear to guide the people during the critical moments of every national regeneration.

The advocates of peace prevailed, and the war party resigned from the government and rose in rebellion, so that those who remained in power were often obliged to inflict the penalty of death upon their erstwhile dearest friends. The Mikado, always for peace, not only forbade any expedition against Korea, but cultivated her friendship. In 1876 a treaty of amity was signed, in which we recognized the full sovereignty of the Hermit Kingdom and for the first time

opened for her commercial relations with the rest of the world. Thus began our open-door policy in the far East. Our object in renouncing our rights over a tributary kingdom was to force China to do likewise and thus create a neutral zone between the two nations. If China and Russia had respected the independence of Korea, no wars would have taken place.

The war with China in 1894-95 was brought about by the ambition of China to make herself the practical owner of Korea, which she claimed as a tributary state. To the ancient pride of China the treaty of 1876 by which we recognized the independence of Korea was a heavy blow. She deeply resented the action of Japan in placing that kingdom beyond the pale of her dominion. Her conservative instincts revolted against oiu-

modernization, and she sought to humiliate that upstart nation which was so insignificant compared with her in point of size. The situation resembled that between Austria and Prussia in the last century, before the Seven Weeks' War, and was practically the outcome of a family quarrel which had to be settled once for all. The parallelism may be still further followed in the internal division of Austria and Hungary and that of Manchuria and China proper, for it should be remembered that the belligerent party was centered around the Manchurian court at Peking and the viceroys of Northern China, whereas the southerners were but lukewarm, even dehghting in the Japanese successes. In this may be found one of the causes for the easy defeat of China at our hands.

The long-sought opportunity for seizing the control of Korea was offered to China in the discord of the Korean government. Here again the antagonism of the cabinet and the household, so fatal to Eastern autocracy, was the real cause of all trouble. To the enlightened statesmen of Seoul the opening of the country and the proposed development of her resources were matters of great satisfaction. The ladies of the household, however, feared the loss of their privileges in the liberal form of government which the cabinet was eager to establish. The household appealed to China for support, while the progressive cabinet sought the aid of Japan. A diplomatic duel ensued, which, as usual, resulted in the victory of the ladies. Practical control over the Korean government was obtained by China in the

year 1894, and she decided to install herself permanently in the peninsula by sending thither, in spite of our protests, a large body of troops. The history of the war is well known. Ping-yang was another Sadowa, and our army conquered the whole of southern Manchuria, including Port Arthur. In 1895 a peace was signed, by the terms of which China fully recognized the independence of Korea and ceded to us Formosa, together with the territories which we occupied at the end of the war. By this treaty we had attained the object of our camjiaign, which was the protection of the territorial integrity of Korea as a safeguard against any further danger from China. With virtual command of the Yellow Sea our anxiety was set at rest.

It was then that the triple coalition

interfered with the just fruits of our victory. In the name of peace, Russia, upheld by Germany and France, forcibly demanded that we give up our newly acquired possessions in Manchuria. This unexpected blow was a severe one, considering the great sacrifices we had made in the war. We were, however, in no position to refuse the combined demands of the three powers, and had only to submit; moreover, as their intervention came in the sacred name of peace, the nation had to be content. The fact that the Muscovite empire soon after coolly took possession of Port Arthur, which she had asked us to evacuate, seemed a queer proceeding; but we offered no opposition to her action, for, as novices in European diplomacy, we still believed in international morality and relied on the fair words of the Russians

when they declared that their intention was to hold that place merely in the interests of universal commerce. Nine years elapsed, during which their real designs became revealed. The greatest shock came to us, however, when we found that they were determined not only to possess Manchuria, but also to annex Korea. Protest after protest was made on our part. Promise after promise was given by Russia, never to be fulfilled. Meanwhile, she was pouring huge armies into Manchuria, and her advance-guard entered Korea itself. The throat of the dragon was touched, and we arose. Among the crags of Liao-tung and the billows of the Yellow Sea we closed in deadly conflict. We fought not only for our motherland, but for the ideals of the recent reformation, for the noble heritage of classic culture,

and for those dreams of peace and harmony in which we saw a glorious rebirth for all Asia.

Who speaks of the Yellow Peril? The idea that China might, with the aid of Japan, hurl her hosts against Europe would be too absurd even to notice were it not for those things from which attention is drawn by the utterance. It may not, perhaps, be generally known that the expression " Yellow Peril" was first coined in Germany when she was preparing to annex the coast of Shantimg. Naturally, therefore, we become suspicious when Russia takes up the cry at the very moment when she is tightening the grasp of her mailed hand on Manchuria and Korea.

The Great Wall of China, the only edifice on earth of sufficient length to be seen from the moon, stands as a monu-

mental protest against the possibility of such a peril. This ancient rampart, stretching from Shan-hai-kuan to the Tonkan Pass, was erected not only as a barrier against foreign encroachment, but also as the self-defined territorial limit of Celestial ambition. During the twenty-one centuries of its existence but occasional sorties were made through its gates, and those only with the object of chastising predatory tribes. It is a fact peculiarly worthy of note that the legendary lore of the Chinese contains no tale of over-sea or crusade-like enterprises, no account of Macedonian conquests or Roman triumphs. The epics of the Trojan war or the Viking sagas find no echo in the literature of the Flowery Kingdom. This cry of a Yellow Peril must, indeed, sound ironical to the Chinese, who, through their traditional policy of non-resistance, are even now suffering in the throes of the White Disaster.

Again, the whole history of Japan's long and voluntary isolation from the rest of the world makes such a cry ridiculous. However changed modern ^o.uC-5^ conditions may be, there is no reason for supposing that either Japan or China might suddenly develop a nomadic instinct and set forth on a career of overwhelming devastation.

If the wont of history is to repeat itself, if a real peril is again to threaten the world, it will be one born in the historic cradle of the steppes, not in the rich valleys of the Hwang-ho and the Yang-tse-kiang, nor on the terraced hillsides of the Japanese archipelago. It was from within the limits of imperial Russia that in ancient times the Goths, the Vandals, the Huns, and the Mongols descended, with their nomadic hosts, over Europe and southern Asia. It is among the tall grasses that wave to the wind from the banks of the Amur to the foot of the Ural Mountains that the Siberian Cossacks and Tartars, grim descendants of Jenghiz and Tamerlane, still roam untamed. In the atrocities committed in Peking and Manchuria, and in the recent horrors of Kishinef, the world may see what is to be expected from the Muscovite soldiery when once their savage nature has broken loose. Russia herself is responsible for the possibility of that peril which she now attributes to the peaceful nations of the far East. When will wars cease? In the West international morality remains far below the standard to which individual morality has attained. Aggressive nations have no conscience, and all chivalry is forgotten in the persecution of weaker races. He who has not the courage and the strength to defend himself is bound to be enslaved. It is sad for us to contemplate that our truest friend is still the sword. What mean these strange combinations which Europe displays,— the hospital and the torpedo, the Christian missionary and imperialism, the maintenance of vast armaments as a guarantee of peace? Such contradictions did not exist in the ancient civilization of the East. Such were not the ideals of the Japanese Restoration, such is not the goal of her reformation. The night of the Orient, which had hidden us in its folds, has been lifted, but we find the world still in the dusk of humanity. Europe has taught us war; when shall she learn the blessings of peace?

THE END

Henry Cabot Lodge

THE AWAKENING
OF JAPAN

BY
OKAKURA–KAKUZO
AUTHOR OF "THE IDEALS OF THE EAST"

NEW YORK
THE CENTURY CO.
1904

Copyright, 1904, by
THE CENTURY CO.

Published November, 1904

THE DEVINNE PRESS

Printed in Great Britain
by Amazon